SCANDALOUS LONDON

Books 1-3

TAMARA GILL

Scandalous London
Books 1-3

~

A Gentleman's Promise
A Captain's Order
A Marriage Made in Mayfair

Copyright 2016 by Tamara Gill

This book is a work of fiction. The names, characters, places, and incidents are products of the writer's imagination or have been used fictitiously and are not to be construed as real. Any resemblance to persons, living or dead, actual events, locales or organizations is entirely coincidental.

All rights reserved. Without limiting the rights under copyright reserved above, no part of this publication may be reproduced, stored in or introduced into a database and retrieval system or transmitted in any form or any means (electronic, mechanical, photocopying, recording or otherwise) without the prior written permission of both the owner of copyright and the above publishers

ISBN: 9781980770466

KEEP IN CONTACT WITH TAMARA

Tamara loves hearing from readers and writers alike.
You can contact her through her website
www.tamaragill.com
or email her at tamaragillauthor@gmail.com.

DEDICATION

For those who love a little scandal in their life...

A GENTLEMAN'S PROMISE

Scandalous London, Book 1

Against her better judgement, Charlotte King bows to family duty and marries a man who is not as he seems. Now trapped in a marriage of the worst kind, her life is an endless cycle of pain and fear. That is until Lord Helsing shows her another way to live...

Lord Mason Helsing walked away from the one woman he'd always cared for, but upon returning to London, he finds Charlotte is in a loveless and cruel marriage. Should he throw away the principles by which he lives and follow a different path than he ought?

But divorce for Charlotte means ruination. And Mason is relied upon to marry well and continue his family. Can they overcome the strictures of society and live the life they've always wanted? Or will they bow to pressure and do as society deems appropriate?

CHAPTER 1

Charlotte waded out into the lake that ran behind her father's Somerset estate and swam toward the middle of the pond. The chilled water cooled her skin and was a welcome reprieve from the scorching summer heat, which England was experiencing that year.

Heat bore down on her head from the sun and she shrugged off the thought that she would freckle. It mattered little what she looked like anymore. Her future was as set as the seasons. The water was a refreshing change after a morning stuck in the stifling hot drawing room with Mama, going over invitations for the forthcoming season in London. Not that Charlotte cared who called or invited them to their events. Her father's decision was made and the marriage contracts were signed.

Charlotte floated onto her back and looked up at the endless blue sky above her. Not a cloud marred the horizon to hint a break in the endless heat wave. Not that she minded, for as long as this hot weather held, the longer her mama would demand that they stay in Somerset. And the longer she could remain unmarried.

The sound of a branch breaking underfoot pulled her from her musings and Charlotte treaded water while trying to find the source of the noise. *Please let it not be Gus.* Her eleven-year-old cousin was the most annoying, vexing boy. Forever reminding Charlotte that he was her father's heir and the future master of her home once the estate passed into his hands, following the demise of her father.

The little rascal seemed to forget she would be long married by then and that he wasn't inheriting a title, merely land, and a home. Little tyrant. Heir or not, she sometimes had the urge to bend him over her knee and spank him until he howled.

"Apologies, Miss King. I did not realize that you were swimming. Forgive my intrusion."

Charlotte shut her mouth with a snap at the sight of Lord Helsing's naked abdomen. His skin glistened and sweat beaded down the middle of his chest, just waiting for the cool spring water to wash it away.

Still unable to speak, her attention wavered to his lordship's skin-tight breeches, which were very snug indeed...Charlotte turned away and splashed some water on her face, hoped that the heat she felt beneath her skin was solely from the sun and not from seeing the man standing behind her on the bank.

"No apology required, my lord. Being as hot as it is today, I had thought to come for a cooling dip." She paused and wondered what he thought of her staring at him. Hoped against hope he did not realize what a profound reaction she always had when she was around him. Her stomach twisted into knots and her mouth dried, usually resulting in her inability to form words. Blushing was the least of her problems.

"Well, I will take your leave. Good day, Miss King."

Charlotte turned about, savoring the vision of his back, which was indeed as pleasing as his front. "I was just about to leave. You may stay and swim if you wish."

His dark, hooded gaze fixed on her and Charlotte fought not to die of embarrassment. They had been friends once. Had in fact been neighbors since they were children. But school and social circles soon placed a wedge between their friendship. As was the case for many children in such circumstances.

"If you're sure, Miss King? I wouldn't wish to impose upon you."

"If my lord would be kind enough to turn for a moment to afford me some privacy, I could emerge from the water," she said, swimming toward the shore.

Lord Helsing turned around and waited for her. Charlotte wrung out her soaked shift as best she could before pulling on her summer gown that buttoned up at the front. Her dress clung to her and was uncomfortable against her skin but she ignored it. The fact that Lord Helsing, one of the most popular gentlemen in town was making conversation with her was too good an opportunity to believe.

"I'm ready, my lord."

Lord Helsing looked over his shoulder and met her gaze. He smiled and turned before making his way to the bank of the lake and sitting started to take off his boots. Charlotte watched as he slid his stockings off, his long feet oddly different to hers. She'd never seen a man's feet before.

"Do you mind if I take a swim, Miss King?" he asked, his brows raised.

Charlotte shook her head and then cleared her throat. "No, of course not."

Charlotte bit her lip as she watched his lordship dive

under the water before emerging with a sigh of pleasure. A well-muscled arm came out of the water and pushed back a lock of hair that had fallen over his brow and the breath in her lungs seized. Never had she been so close to a man only half dressed, not to mention a man who unsettled her with just a glance.

"Delightful," he said.

She couldn't have worded her thoughts better.

"I thought you would be in town, Miss King. Is this not your debut year?"

Charlotte hid her stockings in her pocket and looked about for her shoes. "We're due up any day. As soon as this dratted heat abates, Mother will take me to London." She frowned. "I'm engaged to be married, my lord. Did you know?"

He swam toward the bank, the shock of her statement easy to read on his features.

"I had not heard. Congratulations." He paused. "May I ask who the lucky fellow is?"

"Viscount Remmick, my lord." Charlotte watched to see if Lord Helsing showed some sort of reaction to her words. Or more truthfully, hoped he would. Yet, his easy smile at her words dashed any hopes she may have had that he may have found the news unacceptable. Hopes that he would, in fact, run from the water, pick her up and declare his undying love to her.

Instead, he swam back into the centre of the pond and dived out of sight. By the time he had resurfaced, Charlotte was ready to leave.

"It was a pleasure to see you again, my lord. It had been a long time. I hope we may meet again in town?"

"I may see you tomorrow as I have business with your father. But if not, perhaps our paths will cross in London as you say."

Charlotte discreetly drank in one last sight of him before she turned and walked away. Made sure that she didn't look back. Not once.

CHAPTER 2

Mason handed his horse to the waiting groom and looked up at the red brick Tudor mansion which Charlotte called home. Granted the house was not as grand as his estate, Dellage, but it was beautiful, with the ivy vines and hollyhocks that grew wild on and around its base.

He breathed in deep the smells of a home he knew as well as his own and hoped the missive he'd sent around yesterday to call on Mr King had been received.

Mason met the welcoming gaze of the footman, who opened the door. "Lord Helsing to see Mr. King," he said. The cooling air of the foyer was a welcome reprieve from the heat outside.

The footman having not taken two steps, stopped when Mr King, a tall, stout man, stepped out of the library. When he was young, Charlotte's father used to scare him with his size and boisterousness, but not anymore. Now, the older gentleman seemed jolly instead of daunting. Welcoming instead of annoyed at his presence.

"Welcome, my lord. Please," Mr King said, gesturing him toward the library. "Join me."

Mason followed Mr King into the room. Books littered the walls, along with scrolls and papers placed on any available surface. Unable to see a chair under the assortment of paper work, Mason stood before the desk instead. Mr King laughed and picked up the papers from a chair, allowing him to sit.

"Thank you," Mason said, taking a seat.

"What brings you to our humble establishment, my lord? I hope everything is well at Dellage." Mr King sat behind his desk and steepled his fingers over his rotund stomach.

Mason cleared his throat. "Very well, thank you, no reason for concern on that score," he replied. "No, my business today involves your daughter, Miss King. It's come to my attention she's to marry Lord Remmick and I'm here as an old family friend and neighbor to urge you caution and perhaps persuade you to break the marriage contract."

Mr King sat shocked into silence, his face an awful pasty-white color that didn't bode well for the gentleman's health.

"Are you unwell?" Mason asked, becoming concerned when Charlotte's father reached out for his brandy, downing it in one gulp.

Mr King coughed. "Confused is all. How is it you care what Charlotte does and who she marries? You do understand she has been promised these past two months to Viscount Remmick. It's a little late for neighborly concern now."

Mason nodded. "I've been away on my estates and came home as soon as I'd heard the rumor. I had hoped your daughter would make a more suitable match, and with all due respect, Mr King, Lord Remmick is not." The thought of the lovely Charlotte married to a rogue and one whose past was as sketchy as his health sent shivers of revulsion down his spine.

"Lord Remmick met Charlotte in London before her debut and travelled down here and proposed only two months past. She accepted him, of course. How is it," Mr King said, rising from his chair to refill his brandy glass, "that an Earl, no matter how close a neighbor, would care what my daughter did with her life? We have not entertained in the same circles and I have not seen much of you since you left for Eton and then Cambridge. It does seem odd that you should take an interest now, my lord."

Mason took a moment to gather his wits. His mind whirred with the truth of Mr King's words. True, he hadn't had a lot to do with his neighbors in recent years, but that didn't change the fact that Charlotte had been his closest childhood friend. They were no longer as close as they had been due to the fact they'd grown up, moved in different circles and had vastly different friends, but that didn't mean he did not care for her.

"My lord?" Mr King prompted.

Mason took a calming breath and met the speculative eyes of Charlotte's father. "I suppose as children, when my parents were alive and we stayed at Dellage, a friendship formed between Miss King and myself. I care for her and do not wish to see her hurt in any way. My concern stems from my knowledge of Lord Remmick. He is unsuitable match for Charlotte."

"Charlotte, my lord? You mean, Miss King."

Mason refused to squirm under Mr King's inquisitive stare. "Of course, Miss King," he said.

Mr King sat back in his chair and sighed. "You are asking me if Charlotte can rescind her agreement due to the fact Lord Remmick does not meet your standard of husband for her."

"That is exactly what I'm asking. I'm sure you've heard the rumors about Lord Remmick. Now, I'm not the type of man to sully another's reputation, but when it comes to your daughter's choice in husband, I think it only right I let you know the rumors are true. To think of Miss King subjected to his way of life would be something I would not wish on such a gentle and sensitive young woman." Mason watched surprise then distaste flow over Mr. King's visage. He was aware that the way he was speaking was very insulting to Charlotte's betrothed and could be termed forward at best, yet Charlotte deserved better than a marriage filled with immoral behavior, mostly achieved around the streets and lanes of Covent Garden and the Cyprians who paraded their wares there.

"The contracts have been signed. There is nothing to be done. Charlotte will be Viscountess Remmick by the end of the season. I'm confident my daughter is happy with her choice." Mr. King rang a bell on his desk and stood. "I understand your concern, my lord. But I think as her father that I know what is best for her. She will be in safe and loving hands I assure you."

Mason remained seated, tried and failed at keeping his opinions to himself. "I apologize if you think I've spoken out of turn, but when the happiness of your daughter is at risk, I'm sure you wouldn't wish to ignore my concerns. Are you not the least worried by Lord Remmick's seedy lifestyle? He's a rogue. A man rumored to have caught an unspeakable infection. How could you give your permission, Mr. King?" Mason felt his temper getting away from him and he took a calming breath.

Mr. King waved the footman away who came in at the raised voices. He sighed. "It was her choice. I've always raised my children to be of independent thought. Lord Remmick asked for her hand and Charlotte said yes, it was simple as that." Mr King smiled, the action bordering disdain. "I am aware of his misdemeanors and he has promised to remedy his lifestyle. That is enough for me."

Mason snorted. "And you believed him." He paused and ran a hand through his hair. How could the fellow be so blind? "Does Charlotte know he's poor? He may be titled but all but his pockets are for rent." Mason caught a flicker of anger in Mr. King's eyes, although whether over his questioning or enlightening of Lord Remmick's situation he couldn't tell.

"She knows. Fortunately for Charlotte, her dowry will amply provide for them both and therefore there is no reason for concern. Now, if you'll excuse me, my lord, I have a luncheon with my family to attend."

Mason stood. "This is a mistake. You're letting your eldest daughter make the biggest blunder of her life. I hope, Mr King, that she doesn't live to regret her choice." He walked out of the room without another word. The man didn't seem to have any principles. It made Mason wonder if they'd really told Charlotte the truth of Lord Remmick's situation.

He opened the front door and started when the man himself stood at the threshold about to tap the knocker. "Lord Remmick," Mason said, stepping past him.

His lordship smiled and turned. "Lord Helsing, I was unaware that you were to join us for luncheon."

"I'm just leaving," Mason said, relieved to see his horse being led from the stable.

"Please, do not leave on my account." Lord Remmick laughed. "You know, given enough blunt I'm always willing to share." His lordship winked, before stepping inside.

Mason stood still in shock before anger thrummed hot

in his veins along with helplessness. Charlotte's marriage to that fiend was not what she deserved. He shook his head. Her father ought to be horsewhipped.

He cantered down the graveled, maple-lined drive and images of Charlotte, the sweet, young woman, as pure as a breath of spring air beneath the filthy, diseased rogue haunted him. He pushed his horse into a gallop. He should have courted her himself. At least then she would have the life she deserved. He chastised himself that he hadn't sought her out in London. But never had it occurred to him that she would accept the first marriage proposal she received. It was not uncommon for women to have two seasons before they made their choice. Mason sighed, knowing why she had done so. Charlotte had always been impatient, ready to do and experience everything she could. It would seem she included marriage on her list of many things to achieve early.

He could always bribe Lord Remmick to walk away. Maybe even talk Charlotte into breaking the contract. He was nearing thirty and it was time he thought of marrying. And he knew Charlotte better than any other woman. They would get along well enough.

But Remmick was selfish. It would only be a matter of time before he was back and demanding more funds, until nothing was left of his or Charlotte's fortune. Helsing swore and spurred his horse on.

He would have to let her go and hope for the best. To avoid any uncomfortable meetings, he would close up Dellage and leave for London. Travel in the cool of the evening to limit the strain on his horse. He would not return to Somerset until after Miss King was married and settled.

Happily so, with any luck.

CHAPTER 3

"Was that Lord Helsing I just saw, leaving in a cloud of dust?" Charlotte placed her gloves on her father's desk and poured herself a cup of lemonade. The cool, sour drink went some way towards bringing her body temperature down. Not wholly due to the extreme heat which summer was bestowing on them, but from the view of Mason's departing backside as he galloped down the drive on his horse.

"Yes, it was," her father replied. "I've just had the oddest conversation with the man. It seems he has concerns with whom you've agreed to marry."

"That is exactly what I wished to speak to you about." Charlotte came to stand before him. "I do not think Lord Remmick and myself are well suited. I received a letter today from Amelia, Lady Furrow and not to be impolite papa, she mentioned some terrible rumors going around London in relation to my betrothed. I don't wish to make a mistake."

Her father laughed. "You're just confused, my dear. Should I break the contract and grant you your wish, will you come to me in three months and say the same thing about some other gentleman who asks for your hand? The contracts are signed and to break a contract would be scandalous, not to mention, too expensive, even for me."

Charlotte started at her father's insight. Was she just experiencing wedding jitters, as some women had mentioned to her? Perhaps, yet sometimes, deep in Lord Remmick's eyes she noted an emotion that left her fearful and uneasy. Not to mention her friend's letter and the rumors, some of which made her blush.

Her father sighed. "You'll see, my dear" he said standing. "Lord Remmick is a vibrant, kind, sort of gentleman. He'll treat you well and keep you amused. Trust me," her father said, kissing her cheek just as the library door opened.

"Ah, Lord Remmick, so glad you could join us today."

Charlotte whirled around having been unaware that his lordship was to join them. He wasn't a man usually swayed to venture out of the city. And yet here he was. He strolled toward them like a man without a care. And Charlotte supposed that now her dowry was only a wedding ceremony away, he didn't have any.

Today he was dressed in a bottle green double-breasted coat and nankeen breeches, with shining black top-boots. Lord Remmick looked like a dandy who should be strolling the lawns of Hyde Park instead of her father's library. And although not an overly tall man, his roguish charm often turned heads at balls and parties. Even Charlotte had to admit that when she'd first met him, his quick wit, carefree laugh and perfect attire had bedazzled her. Perhaps she'd imagined that look in his eye that threw shivers of dread down her spine. For the gentleman before her was all charm and finesse.

"My lord Remmick. Welcome to our home." Charlotte curtsied. "I'm so glad you decided to join us."

His lordship flopped himself down on to a chair and started to pull off his gloves. "Well, how could I refuse an invitation to dine with my future family? London is not so very far away. I'll be back in the capital by tomorrow night as it is."

"So soon?" she asked. "Perhaps you could extend your stay with us for a day or two?" Which would enable her to study him more closely, away from the ton and all its diversions. His look of horror at her suggestion put paid to her idea.

"Alas, I cannot. Apologies, Mr. King, Charlotte. But I really must be in London by tomorrow."

"Well, that is a shame, my lord." Her father beckoned toward the door. "The lunch gong has sounded. Shall we?"

Lunch was uneventful. Lord Remmick spoke endlessly of London life and the balls Charlotte would soon be attending with him. Night after night stretched before her, an endless parade, it seemed, of entertainments that he expected her to enjoy along with him.

Nervousness caused butterflies to flutter in her stomach. Although not unaccustomed to the ton and their ways, Charlotte couldn't help feeling a little like a trophy, an ornament that had filled his pockets with coin. After a lengthy discussion on the improvements he would do to their London townhouse and his Surrey estate, Charlotte had heard enough for one day.

"If you'll forgive me, father. But I seem to have a headache. I think I'll lie down for a little while."

Her mother looked up from her syllabub dessert. "Are you alright, my dear? Would you like me to order a tisane for you?"

"That would be lovely. Thank you, mama." Charlotte stood and curtsied. "I will see you all a little later."

"I look forward to it."

Charlotte started at Lord Remmick's lowered tone and piercing gaze that seemed more like a wish to devour her later than to just see her.

She walked slowly upstairs and on reaching her room, received her tisane. While her maid helped her undress, her mind turned to Lord Helsing only a few short miles away. Was he right at this moment undressing that fine, masculine body and crawling into his silk sheets to sleep away the hot afternoon? Not that she knew what type of linen he had, but one could dream.

Charlotte dismissed her maid and locked the door, not trusting Lord Remmick to adhere to the rules of no touching before marriage. And marry his lordship she would. Brought up to believe and trust in her father, she felt he would not lie to her when stating that his lordship was worthy of her hand. That he would be a kind and loving husband.

And it was a little late to worry over her choice now. She'd always been prone to acting hastily. A terrible fault which her mother had forever been trying to banish from her eldest daughter, since she was a child.

What a shame Lord Helsing hadn't approached her the previous season. To come up to her and ask her to dance. To talk to her as they'd talked together as children. Her future could have been very different indeed, had he courted her instead. But he hadn't and now she was promised to another. It would be wrong of her to break the understanding. She would marry Lord Remmick at the beginning of the next season and she would wish Lord Helsing happiness with whomsoever he chose.

CHAPTER 4

Two Years Later – Bath

Mason screwed up the letter from his cousin Amelia, Lady Furrow, and swore. He threw the missive into the fire and sat at his desk to hasten a reply. Anger thrummed through his veins that he'd been correct two years before and that his fears had been realized.

Poor, Charlotte!

"Problem?" His friend George, Lord Mountbatten asked from the settee on which he lay, his cravat untied and his hair mussed from lack of sleep.

Mason sighed and blotted the missive closed. "Yes. I've had a letter from my cousin with some distressing news of an old neighbor of mine. I have to return to London."

George sat up. "When? You can't miss Lady Lancer's ball. Her ladyship will never forgive you."

"It's probably best I leave in any case. Her daughter has been making advances that I'm not reciprocating, if you get my meaning."

His friend laughed. "I understand perfectly well…unfortunately."

Mason stood and rang for a servant. He looked down at his friend and wondered how he could get him to leave without being rude. For weeks George had used his library as a sleeping quarter. Having arrived in Bath he had taken up residence with Mason for a short duration which had turned into a month's long stay. "Why don't you go up to one of the guest rooms," he said. "You're more than welcome to stay and not use my settee as your bed."

"I should return to my father's townhouse. I apologize for being a hindrance. But whenever I'm at home, mama is bothering me with the names of ladies she wishes me to meet. My head spins with the amount she says are worthy of me."

A footman entered and Mason gave him the missive and instructions on his departure early the following morning. He would be back in the capital in a day or so and would see for himself if what Amelia had written was true.

He smiled at the thought of Charlotte and wondered if she'd changed in the years since he'd seen her last. Having married Lord Remmick he hadn't let his mind wonder as to how she was. But now... Now he could not stay away.

Bath was beautiful, and although the society was limited, it afforded him time to make his choice. Unfortunately, he hadn't found the woman he'd wanted to marry here, but the season was young and travelling back to London would widen the possibilities. First, though, he had to ensure Charlotte wasn't as Amelia stated in her letters.

The thought she may be unhappy sent a chill down his spine. A woman of such beauty, inside and out, deserved only the best and he would ensure she was treated with such and nothing else.

"Who was it you said wrote to you from London?"

Pulled from his thoughts, Mason met the inquisitive gaze of his friend. "Lady Furrow, my cousin."

"You're up to something. I want to know what"

Mason sat on the settee across from George. "I'm not up to anything. Not yet at least. Ask me again when I see you in town."

"You have that look about you that I haven't seen since you were plotting the comeuppance of our old professor in Cambridge. Tell me."

"I will tell you nothing. Now go home before your mama comes looking for you. It wouldn't be the first time."

George groaned. "I'm leaving" he said sitting up and tidying his hair. "I have to pack my things."

"What for? Where are you off to now?" Mason asked.

"London. I can't have you having all the fun in town while I'm up here without anyone to keep me amused. Where's the fun in that?"

Mason laughed. "For what I have planned, 'fun' isn't a term I'd use."

"Better and better."

Mason watched as his closest friend waved and walked out the door. He stood and poured himself a brandy and watched as the flames licked at the wood. He would miss Bath and its quieter society. This home and the staff who kept the townhouse ready for him all year round. For the past two years the break from London and the ton was a welcome reprieve. But all good things must come to an end and unfortunately, his time here had as well.

London called as so too did his need to ensure that his childhood friend was safe, happy and being treated in the way all women should be treated. With respect.

CHAPTER 5

London

The crack across Charlotte's jaw knocked her over and left her splayed upon the Aubusson rug. For a moment, blackness was all she could see, before the reality of what her husband, James, had done brought her back to consciousness.

She sat up and took a calming breath. Would not, no matter how many times he assaulted her, let him see her cry.

"Are you happy? See what you made me do," he said coming over and pulling her to her feet. He sat her on the end of the bed and clasped her jaw in a punishing grip.

Charlotte swallowed her fear and helplessness. She'd married a monster, camouflaged behind a suit and top hat. She remained quiet as he inspected what his actions had done to her face.

"You're not fit to be seen in public now. You'll stay home and miss Lord and Lady Furrow's ball. I'll make your excuses." James stood and went to stand before her dressing table mirror. Charlotte watched him fix his cravat and run a hand through his hair. To anyone else, he looked handsome, regal and in control of his life. But he was not. He was the ugliest man she had ever known. A man who could not control the disease inside of him that made him cruel and rotten to the core.

"Amelia will ask questions if I'm not there. Perhaps you should have thought of that before you struck me."

He cast a dismissing glance and walked to the door. "She will not or I'll smack that bitch across the face as well. Or threaten to tell her husband of our affair."

Charlotte gasped. "You lie. Amelia would never betray Lord Furrow."

James grinned. "Of course she wouldn't, but he's a jealous and doting husband. Weak when it comes to his beautiful wife. It would not take much for me to plant the seed of disloyalty and for it to fester under his skin. No matter if it were true or false."

Charlotte watched him go, then walked over to her toilette and dampened a cloth to hold against her face. A dull ache ran through her jaw and a headache began to thump at her temples.

She caught her reflection in the mirror across the room and what she saw left her ashamed. How could her life have turned out so wrong? From the first night of her marriage to James, she'd noticed his personality change.

No longer was he attentive and loving, but indifferent and dismissive. He'd cancelled their wedding trip to the continent, stating he'd not felt up to such a lengthy journey. Instead they'd travelled to London where Charlotte was dropped off at their Grosvenor Square townhouse, while her husband took himself off elsewhere.

After that, endless nights of his drunkenness had occurred. And when she'd chastised him over his behavior and conduct he'd hit her for the very first time.

Her life had continued down that same vein. Of course, Charlotte had learnt not to say anything anymore, for fear that one day he'd strike her so hard she wouldn't wake up.

Sometimes she wished she would not.

Tears streamed down her cheeks and she swiped them away, anger replacing helplessness and shame.

"My lady, do you wish me to help you undress for bed?"

Charlotte looked up and nodded for her maid to enter. The servants had long ago learnt to live with their quick-tempered master. Like Charlotte, they stayed away from his lordship and went about their jobs, making sure they were thorough with their duties lest his lordship was displeased.

"Can you have a tisane made up for me? And bring up a cup of tea before you retire for the night."

"Yes m'lady."

Stripping down to her chemise, Charlotte crawled into bed and wondered what she could do to change her circumstances. Divorce wasn't an option, but she supposed she could always just leave. But then James would win. Would in fact have everything she had brought to the marriage. All her money.

Charlotte thumped the quilt, frustration boiling in her blood. If only he would die. Then all her problems would be solved. But no matter what type of debauchery he lived in the bowels of London, he hadn't yet angered the wrong type of people. Probably because, she mused, he *was* the wrong type of people.

Charlotte thanked her maid as she placed the tisane and tea on the side table. There was nothing she could do besides try and make the best of a terrible situation and hope one day James would change. She drank down the tisane then picked up her tea, taking a sip to remove the unpleasant taste.

She sighed as the sweet brew soothed her a little. Tomorrow was a new day and in three days time she was to attend Lord and Lady Venning's soiree, an event she'd been looking forward to for quite some time.

Not because she was overly close with her ladyship but because Charlotte had found out about one particular guest who was to attend.

It was none other than her childhood friend Lord Helsing. Just the thought of seeing him after such a long time sent excitement through her veins. Would he speak to her or dismiss her? Not since their meeting at her family lake had she seen him. She could have written and kept in contact she supposed, yet whenever she tried, the fear that he would think of her as forward made her throw the letters away instead.

Charlotte finished her tea and sighed. If only she'd stood firm with her father and demanded to be released of the understanding with James, her life could have been be so different now. Not even the blessing of children to take the edge from the life she lived.

Blowing out the candle Charlotte lay down and tried to not feel sorry for herself. She had made her choice, and it had been wrong. It was as simple and unfortunate as that.

※

Lady Venning had outdone herself with her decorations for the soiree. Everywhere Charlotte looked, roses were gathered in bunches around the corners of the room and before the magnificent unlit fireplaces. The evening was warm and the scent was divine, much nicer than the smell of cigars and sweat from having too many people in a room all at once.

Charlotte looked down at her evening gown of dark blue crepe and adjusted her bodice a little. Her fingers shook and she mentally chastised herself for being nervous. Lord Helsing may not even make an appearance. And even if he did, there was no reason for him to seek her out.

After Lord Helsing had left their home that long ago summer's day, he'd changed too. Some would say for the better, if that were at all possible. He had returned to London that following season and thrown himself into the tonnish life with abandon, before taking himself off to Bath to enjoy the small society there.

No longer was he a man who watched life go by before him. Now Lord Helsing enjoyed the ton and all its entertainments. Women spoke of him with wistfulness and affection and Charlotte wasn't naive enough to believe that he ever spent his nights lonely.

Married women spoke of his bedroom exploits and accomplishments as if they were discussing the latest dress patterns in *La Belle Assemblée*. Heat travelled up her neck at the thought and she took a cooling sip of her wine.

Charlotte frowned, pondering on how she'd missed him these past two years. Lord Helsing, it seemed, was determined not to meet her in society, no matter what his words had been the last day they met. But he was in town and no one who was anyone turned down Lord and Lady Venning's invitation. Lord Helsing would be no different.

Charlotte smiled and watched as Amelia strode toward her.

"Charlotte darling, I'm so glad you're here. How are you, dearest?" she asked, giving her a pointed stare.

"I'm fine, truly. I'm sorry I missed your ball." She clasped her best friend's hand.

"You were missed. Your husband made his excuses for you, but I knew as soon as I realized you were not with him what he'd done. I wanted to come and check on you, but Charles wouldn't let me. Not," she said, meeting Charlotte's gaze, "that he wasn't concerned also, but because we were, after all, the hosts."

Charlotte swallowed the lump wedged in her throat over her friend's concern. "Thank you. But I'm better now. In fact, I haven't seen James since he left for your ball. I hope he doesn't arrive here tonight and make trouble."

"He wouldn't dare." Amelia frowned. "Charlotte you know Charles and I would be more than willing to have you stay with us. You need to leave your husband and soon. Before he kills you with his outbursts. This is no way to live your life."

Charlotte bit back her tears. She knew the truth of her situation and Amelia was right. One day James would hit her so hard that she'd never recover. It was only a matter of time. But should she leave, her family would be disgraced, her sisters' prospects shattered like a pane of glass. No, she couldn't leave her husband, even for her own sake.

"You're so kind. And I know how much you care. But I cannot. Please, let's not discuss this now. I'm simply enjoying the freedom of being at a soiree without James hovering over me like a cloak; please let me forget my cares for a little while."

Amelia kissed her cheek. "Of course, darling. Whatever you wish, I'm just concerned for your wellbeing, that's all."

Charlotte smiled. "I know you are. Now, tell me," she said, changing the subject. "How are you feeling? Are the mornings still the worst for you?"

"Yes," Amelia said, placing her hand discreetly on her

belly, as if to guard the little life that grew inside. "The mornings are terrible. Thank goodness I'm well enough in the evenings to attend the season's entertainments. I don't know how I'd survive otherwise."

Charlotte smiled while a pang of envy shot through her. Not once in the two years she'd been married had she bore a living child. It was another reason why James abhorred her. In his eyes, she was a barren, useless piece of common baggage that he should never have married.

When Charlotte had reminded him her common class had saved his estate and him against his debtors, she'd paid for it by being bedridden for a week. The belting he'd inflicted had been one of the worst she'd ever had. And she'd learnt to curb her tongue from that point onwards. As much as doing so irked her greatly.

"Charlotte are you well?"

She started out of her musings and smiled. "Of course, just lost in thought, that's all. What were you saying?"

"Only that Lord Helsing has arrived. And that he's looking directly at you."

Charlotte looked up and locked eyes with Mason immediately. It was almost as if an invisible line connected them across the sea of heads. She smiled and watched as he nodded in greeting before moving off to join another party his side of the room.

"He's as handsome as ever. Why did you never tell me you were neighbors as children? I had to find out about it by Lady Sisily."

Charlotte started at the question having never thought to tell Amelia of their childhood friendship. It was bad enough just to think about Mason and the silly passion she'd once held for him.

"I'm sorry, Amelia. I suppose it slipped my mind. It's been, after all, two years since I saw him last."

Amelia cast her a speculative look, then turned her attention back to the throng. "Well, I suppose you'll be able to catch up tonight. And without Lord Remmick here, I'm sure you'll be able to relax a little and enjoy your reunion."

Charlotte swallowed. It was silly really to be nervous about talking to Lord Helsing again. Granted, they hadn't been close for many years, but after that one day near the lake, everything had changed for Charlotte. He'd been kind and attentive like the old days, something that she longed for her husband to be now. Not that he ever would be.

She caught sight of his lordship strolling through the throng before he asked a young debutante with doe eyes to dance. A pang of jealousy shot through her and Charlotte chastised herself. She was married and he was not. Of course, he could dance with whomsoever he wished.

She watched as he waltzed about the room with the beautiful, young woman, his grace and ease obvious to any who observed. Lord Helsing seemed much broader across the shoulders and his hair was a little less tidy, and yet, to Charlotte, he was the handsomest man present.

"Perhaps it is best that you stop your inspection of Lord Helsing, dearest as your husband just stumbled through the door."

Charlotte watched in horror as James staggered into the room, needing the wall and a few guests for support. His cravat hung about his neck and his shirt gaped open at his throat. He looked sweaty and not at all well. People gasped and moved out of his way as James looked about the room.

For her.

Charlotte stepped away from Amelia and started to walk toward him, thankful the minstrels continued to play and people danced. He stood upright as she came to his side.

"I'm so pleased to see you, dear James." She smiled to hide her distaste. "Amelia and I are over the other side of the room. Come and sit with us there."

He gave her a dismissing look and pulled his arm from her hand. Charlotte let him go and followed as he swayed toward her friend. Embarrassment threatened to choke her. It felt as if everyone watched the spectacle that was their marriage. A prickling of heat suffused her cheeks and Charlotte lifted her chin, not willing to cower under the collective mocking and curious gazes.

James flopped into a chair and sprawled like a man who was about to go to sleep. Charlotte sat beside him, summoning a footman for some water.

"James, you need to sit up. You're at Lord Venning's home and you know how he detests drunkenness and rowdy behavior."

"Bite your tongue, woman. Who are you, a commoner, to tell a Viscount how to behave?"

Amelia sat beside James and smiled. "She has every right, as your Viscountess. Furthermore, your sickly pallor and untidy attire is hardly appropriate for polite society. You ought to be ashamed of yourself embarrassing your wife in such a way, Lord Remmick." Amelia stood. "I will seek you out later, my dear."

Charlotte nodded and waited for James's temper to take hold. Amelia had every right to hate him, why she hated him too now. There was no affection left in their marriage. James had extinguished that the first time he hit her.

"How dare that bitch speak to me so? I ought to—"

"Remember where you are, James." Charlotte handed him a drink. "Sit up and drink this and try and look the gentleman. You do know your cravat is untied?" Charlotte smiled at two passing matrons and tried not to imagine what they must be thinking.

James looked down at his shirt and laughed. "Well, I'll be. Seems I didn't tie it up after. Well, let me just say she had the longest legs, wrapped them nicely about my hips while I gave it to her up against a deserted lane's wall." He smirked and met Charlotte's gaze. "You don't mind do you, my lady. Since you no longer spread your legs for me, I have to find my enjoyment elsewhere."

Charlotte shuddered and looked about to ensure no one was within hearing range. "What you do in your spare time is no concern of mine, but you must, when appearing at social events, at least look like the Viscount you were born to be."

"She was a ripe beauty as well. New to London from up north somewhere. With just one touch I was able to make her as wet as the Thames between her legs. The sweetest woman I've tasted in an age. Would you like to kiss me and find out, my dear?"

"You're a vile, piece of human flesh and I'm ashamed to call you my husband."

James clasped her jaw and Charlotte stilled before he gathered his wits and sat back laughing. "You'll pay for that later."

Tears threatened and Charlotte bit the inside of her lip. Hard. Why wouldn't he just leave? Go back to the cesspit he was so fond of in the East end of town and let her be?

CHAPTER 6

Mason watched Charlotte and Lord Remmick argue from across the room and the blood in his veins ran cold when he saw his lordship clasp Charlotte's delicate jaw as if to hurt her in some way.

He nodded but did not comment on the conversation going on around him, while he waited to see what Lord Remmick would do next. So the rumors were true. Charlotte was in a marriage of the worst kind. If Lord Remmick was willing to grab his wife in public, one shuddered to think of what the man could do behind closed doors.

A simmering anger boiled in his blood at the thought of his childhood friend Charlotte, this beautiful woman she had grown into, being a punching bag for her husband's woes and disappointments.

It was not to be borne.

Mason downed the last of his brandy and strolled toward Charlotte and her husband. He couldn't help but smile when she stood, her large eyes full of welcome and also, he noted, apprehension.

He bowed. "Good evening, Lord and Lady Remmick. It has been a long time."

Charlotte curtsied. "Good evening, Lord Helsing. Indeed it has been a long time. Too long in fact."

Mason looked at Lord Remmick and waited for him to stand and acknowledge him. With a sigh of annoyance, he did so, swaying before Charlotte clasped his arm to keep him from falling over.

"Lord Helsing. We are honored by your presence. Why, I do believe the last time I saw you, you were quite put out." Lord Remmick laughed and splashed some of his water over his shirt. Not that it made any difference, as his lordship's shirt was already marred with stains of suspicious origins.

Mason cast Lord Remmick a dismissive glance and turned his attention back to Charlotte. She was as beautiful as he remembered her and yet something about her had changed. No longer did she seem as carefree and at ease as she once had. The spark that had glowed in her eyes was no longer there. No doubt, due to the fiend she'd married.

"Would you care to dance, my lady? There is to be a cotillion next."

Charlotte smiled. "I would love to, my lord."

"You would love to, my dear?" Remmick said, glaring at her. "What else would you love to do, I wonder? Were you not friends many years ago? And did I not steal her away from under your nose, Lord Helsing? You know my offer still stands."

Mason ground his teeth. Nothing would please him more than to punch the obnoxious bastard on his nose. Another time, he promised himself. "On the contrary, my lord. But you are right with one point. Lady Remmick and myself have known each other all our lives."

"What was the offer, James?" Charlotte asked, frowning.

Mason glared at his lordship, letting him know without words he should keep his mouth shut.

Remmick laughed. "I merely offered to share you, my dear. Of course, Lord Helsing would have to pay for your services. Not," he added, flicking a piece of invisible lint from his coat, "that you are worth very much. Your...abilities shall we say behind closed doors are somewhat...lacking."

Charlotte gasped and turned to walk away. Mason clasped her hand and pulled her onto the floor to dance with him instead. He looked down at her and anger churned in his stomach at her unshed tears.

"How are you, really, Charlotte?" he asked.

"Mortified. I cannot believe James could speak of me, or to you, in that unseemly manner. I'm so sorry."

"Don't be," he said, stepping away from her for a moment before the music brought them back together. "It is not your fault Lord Remmick is a cad. I apologize as he's your husband, but some things are better left unsaid."

Charlotte nodded and a pang of regret pierced Mason's soul. He regretted that he hadn't fought harder for her. Regretted that he hadn't insisted that her father break the contracts and damn the scandal. How could such a beautiful woman, inside and out, be married to the worst debaucher and rake in London.

"I have been watching you for a while and to me you do not have the appearance of a happy woman. Tell me everything is well at home?"

Charlotte paled and missed a step. Mason clasped her about her waist and a longing to hold her assailed him. "Please," he added.

She sighed. "We are perfectly well, thank you. There is nothing for you to worry about."

Mason's gut clenched at the lie. He watched her dance, and although she knew the song well, there was no joy in her eyes. No life.

"You're lying."

Charlotte met his gaze and Mason knew instinctively what type of life she lived. The bastard bashed her. Probably took pleasure in her pain. And she was frightened. This dance with him would probably make Lord Remmick think he had the right to hit her again.

"Truly, my lord. I'm fine. Please do not concern yourself." She cast a nervous glance to where her husband sat and frowned a little.

Mason looked over his shoulder and noted his lordship watching them intently. His visage one of fury. Mason ground his teeth. "You cannot stay married to him," he said. "He'll end up killing you, Charlotte and you know it. You must speak to your father at once."

"Shush," she said, looking about. "I've already told you there is nothing wrong. Now please, let us enjoy what's left of our dance, so we may part as friends."

"I can protect you." Mason gave her a pointed stare that dared her to refute him.

"You can protect me? How? By bringing shame and scandal to both our families? I'm married and there is nothing to be done."

Mason watched her storm from the dance floor just as the music ended. He sighed and looked about for her friend Lady Furrow. Spying her ladyship beside her husband, the Earl, Mason went to join them and to see what exactly could be done to save Charlotte from Lord Remmick and his abusive clutches.

Later that night, Charlotte sat on her bed and nursed the stinging slap James had bestowed on her cheek. It was a relief that his anger over her dancing with Lord Helsing had ended there. On the carriage ride home, he had chastised her endlessly, berated and yelled at her over her 'wantonness' and 'whoring' that, according to him, all of London knew and was talking about.

Sometimes Charlotte actually thought that James was losing his mind. Since their marriage, she'd been nothing but the best wife to him. A wife who tolerated a lot. Not that she had a choice in the matter. There was little anyone could do to make her situation improve.

She heard the front door slam and knew James had left for the night and if anything like his other nights out on town, wouldn't be home for several days. Charlotte rang for some heated water and waited. She sat before her dressing table and stared at her reflection. At twenty years, she was still an attractive woman.

Anger thrummed through her over her husband's violent behavior. Who was he to hit her? And why should she put up with it any longer? The next time he went to strike her would be his last.

Mason's words whispered in her mind, "I can protect you". There was no doubt that he could if she asked him. But other than divorcing Lord Remmick – which she refused to do – there was little to be done. Although, perhaps Mason could help her in another way. In the ways of a man and woman and in one need in particular.

Charlotte pulled the pins from her hair and let her light locks pool about her shoulders. Her dark cobalt blue eyes gave her an air of exoticness that she liked and from the glances which some gentleman had bestowed upon her, she knew that they appreciated her too.

She started when her maid brought in the water and towels. Charlotte dismissed her for the night. She washed thoroughly, then went to her armoire and looked through her clothing. She pulled out a gown that buttoned up at the front and had a hood. It was not something she would normally wear in public, but it was perfect for what she had planned in a certain gentleman's bedroom.

Searching through her chest of drawers she found an almost transparent shift and pulled it over her head. Then picking up the gown, she tied it up over the shift.

Nerves fluttered in her stomach over what she was about to do. Charlotte took a calming breath, pulled the hood over her hair and left her room. Walking down the stairs, she saw the night footman jump to attention as he noticed her and bowed.

"Can I help you, my lady?"

"Can you summon a hackney carriage please? I'm going out."

The footman nodded and ran outside. Charlotte pushed down the desire to run back to her room and forget the folly she'd embarked upon. Then, the thought of her husband and his abusiveness toward her strengthened her resolve. James could very well kill her the next time he was inclined to strike her. She'd be damned she'd die without living first.

The footman came in some minutes later and beckoned her toward the door. Charlotte followed him and took a calming breath of London's still night air. She gave the driver the direction to Lord Helsing's residence and sat back. Excitement over the unknown made her restless and she fidgeted with her reticule.

Would Mason admit her? By his hooded, appreciative

gaze during their dance tonight and his reassuring words she felt that he would. Still, she was married and what she was about to do was an unforgivable transgression. Charlotte supposed she should feel guilty, but all she felt was expectation. Like her body was alive again.

The drive was short and before Charlotte knew it, the cab pulled up beside a Georgian townhouse on Berkeley Square. Lights blazed from a first floor window and two from the second. Until now, she hadn't thought that Mason may still be out or worse, that he may be entertaining someone else... She pushed the dismal thought aside and stepped out onto the pavement. Paying the driver she walked up the short flight of steps and knocked.

Within moments a footman opened the door. His widened eyes told of his shock at seeing a lady dressed in hooded, secretive apparel and standing on the street in the middle of the night. Charlotte walked past him and into the foyer. The home was of similar layout to hers. With a tiled mosaic floor and winding staircase up to the second story, she could almost picture herself back there. Except this home, seemed much more comforting and welcoming than hers ever would.

"I'm here to see, Lord Helsing. Tell him Charlotte King is here. He isn't expecting me."

"If you'll wait here, Miss King."

Charlotte watched as the footman walked toward what she assumed to be the library or front drawing room. She heard muffled voices before rapid footsteps sounded in the adjacent room.

"Charlotte, are you well?" Lord Helsing clasped her hand and studied her for a moment. "What are you doing here?"

"May we speak in private, my lord?"

He frowned and Charlotte could read the confusion in his gaze. "Of course," he said. "Please, follow me."

The room was a library with floor to ceiling paneling and books. The smell of leather and cigars mixed with an old book scent Charlotte had always loved met her senses. She sat down on the settee before the unlit hearth and wondered for a moment if she'd done the right thing.

Pushing back her hood, she watched Mason shut and lock the door before joining her on the chair. Nerves skittered up her arm when he clasped her hand.

"He's hit you hasn't he? And don't lie to me this time. I can see by your reddened cheek that he has."

Charlotte nodded. "He's often violent and cruel. So cruel it's beyond imagining." Tears threatened to spill down her cheeks and she bit her lip. "I should never have married him. Had I known..."

"You weren't to know. I knew he was fond of nightly pursuits in the bowels of London, but I did not know he would hit his wife." He rubbed a tear from her cheek and Charlotte leaned toward his touch. It had been so long since she'd had contact filled with reverence and care with another person. "I should have waited. Married someone else. Anyone but James." She met his gaze and for the life of her, couldn't look away.

"I blame your father as much as I blame your husband. I have not told you this before but the day I came to visit your home, the day after we'd met at the lake I went there for a particular reason."

"Which was?" Charlotte asked frowning. Lord Helsing stood and went to stand before the hearth, watching as the flames licked at the wood. "I lied when I said I hadn't heard of your betrothal. I had. And having heard I set off for home to discuss the matter with your father. I knew of Lord Remmick's...history and thought to warn your father.

Make him see the error in agreeing for you to marry such a cad and therefore break the understanding." Mason paused and a pained expression crossed his visage. "He wouldn't listen." He turned and met her gaze. "I failed you that day. As a friend, a neighbor and as a gentleman."

"You didn't fail me, Mason," she said, using his Christian name for the first time in an age. "I failed myself." Tears pricked her eyes and she sniffed. "When father said you'd come with reservations about Lord Remmick I should have listened. I've know you for so long. We'd played, laughed, fought in the past but you've never placed me in harm's way. I should've taken heed of your doubt and acted on it."

"We all make mistakes, Charlotte. We wouldn't be human if we did not." He came and sat beside her and clasped her hand. "Why are you really here, Charlotte? It's the middle of the night."

A myriad of desires and needs thrummed through her veins at his direct question. Why was she here? Because she'd always loved him. From the moment she'd met him as a young girl, she'd loved him. Charlotte studied Mason's features, his straight nose and aristocratic jaw. His untidy hair that looked as if he'd run his fingers through it too many times. How she loved him.

Charlotte leaned forward and clasped his jaw. He stilled for a moment but didn't pull back as she continued on her quest and kissed him.

When he didn't respond, she sat back and studied his reaction. "I'm sorry. I don't know what I'm doing. I came here tonight to teach James a lesson and all I've ended up doing is making myself look like a fool." She swallowed a sob and searched for a handkerchief in her cloak pocket. She was a ridiculous fool, about to make another mistake to add to her many. Mason was her friend, not a lover.

Why she even thought he would look at her in that way was an absurd notion.

"You need to go home, Charlotte and think about what you wish to do. You're married and if we go down this road, there will be no turning back. For me at least," Mason said, standing and pulling her up. Her cloak opened and she quickly tied it closed again, but not before Mason had seen what scandalous evening wear she had on.

"I understand and you're right. Revenge is never the way to solve a problem, even my problems, as great as they are. I apologize for intruding upon you."

He clasped her jaw and made her look up at him. "I've always cared for you, you know that. Yes, many years passed that we never saw one another, but you were always thought of and wondered about. Do not imagine the reason I'm sending you home stems from my not wanting you. Without a second thought, I would rip that cloak from your shoulders, untie your shift and take you here on this settee and let your husband be damned. But I will not. If you want to be with me it needs to be out of your desire to be with me, not your lust to hurt your husband in any way you can."

Mason led Charlotte out of his townhouse and walked her though his back garden toward the mews. He summoned his stableman to fetch a Hackney and have the cab brought around the back.

"Pull your hood over your hair a little more, Charlotte. I don't want you to be seen leaving my premises." Mason looked toward the street and cursed the blasted Hackney driver for taking his time. Under the moonlight and knowing Charlotte wanted to sleep with him was almost too much to resist.

Almost...

But the thought that she would add him to her list of mistakes kept him rooted to the spot. She needed to come to him out of desire, need or affection...for him alone. But never revenge. He couldn't stomach that.

A tear slid down her cheek and he clamped his jaw. Damn it, he'd never intended to hurt her. The last person on earth he'd ever wish to injure was Charlotte. He pulled her into his arms.

Her willowy figure sat snug against his and he breathed in deep the exotic smell of her hair. "I don't send you away because I want to," he said, rubbing her back and knowing her body was only two pieces of material away. "Please say you understand."

The sound of the coach rumbled on the cobbled drive and Mason pulled Charlotte toward the gate. "Charlotte?"

She nodded and pulled back. "I do. I'm just mortified I humiliated myself."

Mason ran a hand through his hair. "You didn't. Just promise me you'll sleep on what I've said tonight. When you wake in the morning, you'll understand where I'm coming from. But know this, it isn't due to my lack of interest."

She nodded. "Goodnight, Lord Helsing."

Mason helped her into the coach and shut the door. He flicked the driver a sovereign and gave the man Charlotte's address. "Goodnight, my lady," he said as he watched it drive away before turning a corner and going out of view. He swore and stormed back through his garden gate and strode toward his house. For the first time in his life, Mason cursed the fact he'd been born a gentleman and given the airs of one. Next time, he wasn't quite sure he would have it in him to deny Charlotte anything.

Least of all himself.

CHAPTER 7

Mason sat atop his horse and watched as Charlotte galloped down Rotten Row at breakneck speed. A week had passed since he'd seen her, her avoidance of him starting to irritate. The fact she was also out riding without a chaperone grated on his nerves. Since kissing her, as quick and innocent as that kiss was, Mason had cursed his gentlemanly behavior. His gut clenched at the memory and he swore.

Charlotte, un-chaperoned and alone, wasn't safe, not with him around at least.

He cantered toward her and watched as her eyes flared in surprise. "Good morning, Lady Remmick," he said, tipping his head in acknowledgement.

A shade of rose bloomed on her cheeks and he smiled. "Lord Helsing," she replied. "I thought I had this turf to myself this morning, being as early as I am."

"I like to ride early myself. It clears my head." She looked about and shifted on her saddle and Mason wondered what she was thinking. Was she uncomfortable around him now? Did she regret her words and actions of a week earlier? "I have not seen you about. I hope you're well."

"I'm very well, thank you, my lord. The weather is very congenial today, my horse…"

Mason ground his teeth at the benign banter. He sighed. "Charlotte, if we're only ever going to speak about the weather or our horses, our conversation will soon bore even me. And while I like to discuss my cattle as much as any other gentleman, I do wish you would trust me enough to talk to me as a friend."

A pained expression flitted across her features. "I cannot. I'm sorry."

"Yes you can, you just don't want to." He threw her a pointed stare. "Charlotte?" Again she looked about before she met his gaze and raised her chin.

"I'm so sorry about last week. I really don't know what came over me. I'm not usually like that." She bit her lip and his gut clenched. "Please forgive me."

"There is nothing to forgive. You've done nothing wrong. If anything, it is I who owe you an apology."

"Why?" she asked.

"For turning you away."

Charlotte's stomach twisted into delightful knots at Mason's words. For days, she'd chastised herself for a silly fool. Embarrassment over how she'd propositioned him made her squirm daily. Never did she think she could look him in the eye again without dying on the spot. But the gentleman that Mason was, proved her wrong. He read her as easily as a book and knew her reaching out for him was just that. A call to help and comfort when she was down. The fact that he didn't take advantage of her during a time of need spoke volumes as to what kind of man he was.

He was a true gentleman. "I understand why you did and I thank you for doing so. I so wish for us to be friends again. To be as close as we were as children. I've always thought of you and hoped you were happy." Charlotte walked her horse on and smiled when he came abreast. "Tell me about Bath and your time there. When time permits, I really should make a trip up there myself. I have a cousin who lives there did you know?"

"I do know that, yes," he said. "I enjoy travelling and although Bath is not so very far away, the limited society suits me. I'll return there should the season in town prove…"

"Prove what?" Charlotte asked, wondering why Mason looked uncomfortable for the first time since she'd seen him. "Mason, what were you going to say?"

He chuckled. "Prove disappointing. I find now that I'm nearing thirty I should look for a wife if you really must know."

"How diverting," Charlotte said laughing and enjoying herself for the first time in a very long time. "No one caught your fancy? I find that very hard to believe."

"Believe it, my lady for it is true. And not through lack of trying on my behalf. But there was never that…"

"Spark?" Charlotte smiled at him and he nodded.

"Yes, that spark," he replied catching her eye.

Charlotte knew all too well what that spark felt like and to know you were married to a man who didn't raise so much as a flicker of a flame left her hollow. Not to mention that after that fleeting kiss she'd shared with Mason, her whole outlook on love and what a man and woman could share with mutual desire, had altered. For the first time since she'd watched him swim in the lake, she'd desired a man to touch her. To do more than just kiss her. She'd wanted him. Desperately. And none of the emotions resembled revenge. When she thought of passion, she thought of only Mason and not her husband.

"I hope you find it, my lord. There is nothing worse, believe me, than to live a life without that spark."

Mason sighed and pulled his horse to a stop as other riders took to the track just ahead of them. "I do not wish that for you, Charlotte. You're a beautiful woman. A kind and considerate lady who deserves so much more than you've been dealt. Ask me again."

Charlotte shivered at his words and met his gaze. "Ask you what again?" Her voice came out in a rush and she inwardly swore. As if she didn't know just what.

"Ask me."

Mason's voice resonated with steadfast resolve and she tore her gaze away from his. To think straight, she couldn't drown in orbs so blue and swirling with need that she would flounder. But how could she not wade out into murky waters? Not to would mean never to live, experience all that life, this man, was offering her.

"You didn't want me to ask unless it wasn't owing to my seeking revenge," she stated.

"Then make sure it does not. Now ask."

"Will you sleep with me?" The words came out as a rushed whisper, but Mason heard. A muscle on his temple worked as he stared silently at her.

"I don't believe sleep will factor into our agreement, my lady."

Were it possible Charlotte's toes would've curled in her boots. "I hope not."

CHAPTER 8

Charlotte settled against the squabs of her hackney cab and tried to calm her nerves. After meeting Mason in Hyde Park the thought of what they were about to start, to do with each other left excitement thrumming through her veins and expectation right alongside of it. It had taken three days for James to leave. The reason why he could be staying home annoyed and worried her at the same time. Not that she cared what happened to her husband anymore, that part of her conscience had died a long time ago, but maybe he'd caught some awful disease and was sick. And should he force himself on her would make her sick also. She shuddered and tried to calm her racing thoughts. Tonight she needed to concentrate on one man and one man only.

Mason.

The cab pulled up before his town house and she alighted and was ushered inside without having to knock. She smiled and walked toward the library having seen the candlelight flickering from the ajar door.

Mason sat leaning on his knees and staring at the

flames in the hearth. He looked lost in thought, even worried if the slight frown lines beside his eyes were any indication. Charlotte stopped and wondered if he'd changed his mind. Regretted his words.

Please no.

"My Lord?"

Mason stood quickly and came over to greet her. He smiled as he reached over her shoulder and shut the door. "Good evening, my lady."

Charlotte handed him her cloak and laughed. "I'm so nervous. I know I shouldn't be, because you'd never hurt me, but I've never done…"

"Come and sit." He pulled her toward the settee and her hand burned at his touch. She had wondered over the last few days if that spark they spoke of was a figment of imagination, need, on her behalf. But now, right at this moment, with his large hand clamped around hers, she knew such thoughts were untrue. With Mason her whole body reacted, sparked to life like a firecracker ready to explode.

She sat.

"You're very beautiful this evening." Mason ran a finger down her cheek, leaned in and kissed beneath her ear. Charlotte shut her eyes and bit her lip to stop herself from throwing herself into his arms like a crazed, affection starved matron.

"Thank you," she managed.

His lips touched her shoulder and she shivered. "There is no need for thanks."

She clutched the lapels of his coat and pulled him against her. "Mason. Please."

He growled and took her lips in a searing kiss. Finally!

Charlotte moaned as his tongue licked her lips. Heat coursed through her veins when he deepened the embrace;

almost consuming her with his desire. Never had she wanted anyone as much as she wanted Mason to take her here, right now, on his library settee.

"Are you sure?" he said, clasping her hand when it reached the buttons on his frontfalls.

"I have never been more certain of anything." Again, her lips touched his while her hand unbuttoned his breeches. It took some coaxing to slip open his buttons, but eventually the flap opened and she was able to clasp his straining member.

Velvety, soft skin slid against her palm and Mason moaned. Charlotte wrapped her fingers about him and stroked him as he kissed her senseless. Heat pooled at her core and she gasped when his hand kneaded her breast through her dress.

"I want you," she managed to say. Mason quickly unbuttoned the front of her dress, pushing the garment from her shoulders. He pulled back for a moment to pull her transparent shift over her head, leaving her naked.

Cool night air kissed her skin and Charlotte felt her nipples peak into tight buds. She bit her lip at the savagery and desire she could read in his gaze as it locked on her, scorched her. Expectation ran up her spine and she ran her hand over the tip of his penis feeling his desire.

He laid her down onto the settee and settled between her legs. Charlotte gasped as he pushed against her sex and teased her with his body. Her breathing hitched as he watched and continued to taunt her relentlessly.

"I won't want to give you back, Charlotte. There is no denying me if we do this. From this moment on, you're mine and no other's."

Her mind a haze, Charlotte nodded. Would in fact do anything Mason said right at this moment. He pushed a little inside and started to pay homage to her breasts. She ran her fingers through his dark locks and held him there. The wicked things he was doing with his tongue sent sensations to spike toward her core. "Mason please," she begged.

He chuckled and feathered kisses up her neck before kissing her lips with such reverence that Charlotte could almost defy any scandal to come live with him. Divorce James and marry Lord Helsing indeed.

"You are mine." The deep, lust-tinged voice brooked no argument as he thrust into her core and took her. "Always," he said.

She gasped as the size of him took her a moment to accommodate. Fullness and completeness was all she felt. Charlotte wrapped her legs about his waist and a delicious pressure built inside. She clutched at his shoulders and realized with some amusement that he still wore his shirt and pants. The image of her naked and Mason above her, taking her fully clothed made her moan.

"Mason, I'm—"

"Let go, Charlotte."

She met his gaze and bit her lip. Oh, it felt so good. Tighter and tighter she coiled about him, needing to be closer, wanting him harder with every stroke, until a pleasure unlike any she thought possible exploded in and all around her.

"Mason," she moaned into his shoulder. Her body riding his until the last of her orgasm was spent. Mason quickened his pace, his gasp against her ear marking his own orgasm.

They stayed like that for a time, both trying to regain their breath and understanding over what had just happened between them.

Charlotte pulled back and pushed a lock of hair from his face. "That was amazing."

He chuckled. "Yes it was," he said, kissing her again, in a slow, sensuous manner. "And I meant what I said before, Charlotte. I'll not share you."

Charlotte swallowed. "I'm married, Mason. You have to accept that."

The moment he pulled away, she missed his heat. He stood and walked toward the hearth, and Charlotte could tell by the tautness of his shoulders that he was angry. And he had every right to be. But then, he knew why she'd come here for tonight. To seek solace, love from a man she'd always admired and cared for. They were just two people who had freely chosen to love each other. Nothing more could be between them other than friendship and perhaps a repeat of tonight, if he was willing. But no matter how much she wished to divorce James, she could not. The scandal would kill her father, not to mention ruin her sister's hope of marrying well.

Mason ran a hand through his hair. "You deserve better, Charlotte. Leave him and be damned the scandal."

Charlotte came over and clasped his hands. "I know you would support me should I do such a thing. You're the best of men, but I cannot. I don't care about my own reputation, but should I leave James I'd ruin my sister in an instant. My parents would never recover from the shock."

"Do they know how violent James is? Surely your father would not wish you to come to any harm."

"Of course he wouldn't, but no they do not." Charlotte stepped away and started to look for her gown. "He may be cross and talk to James but that would only ensure another beating for me at his hands. I'm married and that is that."

"It's not that." The vehemence behind Mason's tone sent shivers up Charlotte's spine.

She pulled on her dress and started doing up its

buttons. "I know I'm being selfish in wanting you without any recourse or commitment. In fact you may think me fast, a woman best suited for the *demi monde* than the society we grace. But I just wanted you. I've wanted you for so long it, physically hurt." Charlotte took a calming breath. "Let us have some time together, please. If my sister marries then I will leave James as soon as the ink is dry on the marriage register."

Mason stared at her a moment then came and pulled her into his arms. He smelt divine, of sandalwood and her. Charlotte snuggled into his chest and reveled in the beat of his heart.

"So, we're to have a repeat performance of tonight? You are wanton, Charlotte."

She laughed the sound almost foreign to her. "With you I am, my lord. When can I see you again?"

"Are you attending Lord and Lady Wilson's ball tomorrow evening?"

Charlotte nodded, having received the invitation to London's most looked forward to event. Every year his lordship always threw a ball where something happened. Whether it be a betrothal, a performance or special guest, Lord Wilson always had something to keep his guests occupied and happy.

"So? We will speak then."

Charlotte leaned up and kissed him quickly. "I shall miss you."

He growled and swooped her into his arms. "Who said I was ready to let you go?" And he didn't let her go; not until the hour before dawn.

CHAPTER 9

Charlotte couldn't wipe away the smile from her lips as she watched Lord Helsing stroll across the room toward her. Tonight he wore a blue, superfine, long tailed coat with a pristine white shirt and waistcoat beneath. His neckcloth was tied perfectly and only accentuated his handsome visage, very much like his black satin knee-breeches that fit his masculine thighs to perfection. He looked regal and tall, a gentleman with a roguish grin that left her knees weak.

She swallowed as heat coursed throughout her body, remembering what he'd done to her the night before. After seeing him as a man at her father's lake all those years ago, Charlotte had often wondered what he'd be like when intimate with a woman. And now she knew and was anything but disappointed with her findings.

As luck would have it, her husband was still absent since his departure the previous evening, and so tonight, Charlotte was here by herself. Of course, Amelia waltzed about the floor with Lord Furrow, but no longer did she feel the need to impinge on the happily married couple's time. At least not as much as she'd formerly done.

For now, she had another more fascinating companion. Lord Helsing.

"Good evening, Lady Remmick. May I say how beautiful you look this evening?"

The devilish twinkle in Mason's gaze made goosebumps rise across her flesh. Charlotte tapped her fan against his arm and curtsied. "Good evening, my lord."

He came and stood beside her with his hands behind his back before he leaned in and whispered against her ear, "May I also say how delicious you look, Charlotte. Good enough to eat, in fact."

Charlotte refused to blush and instead laughed to cover her nervousness. "Behave." She met his gaze and the heat she read in his eyes made her breath hitch in her lungs.

"I don't want to."

How could just four simple words leave her aching with need? She had, after all only left his bed in the early hours of this morning. And yet, here she was, panting like she'd run about the block in a tightly strung corset. "Then we're in agreement. Although the thing is, my lord," Charlotte said moving closer to his side to ensure privacy, "what are we to do about it?"

Mason took two flutes of champagne from a passing footman and handed one to Charlotte. "Well that is yet to be decided. But I can imagine one thing we'd both enjoy immensely."

Charlotte laughed and took a cooling sip of her drink. "Later?"

He nodded and excitement thrummed in her veins. Were she not married, her urge to clasp his arm and declare to everyone present that he was hers would have been beyond her control. Charlotte pushed away the depressing thought that he wasn't hers and instead turned her attention to the guests at the ball.

The musicians played an elegant piece of music while the dancers moved gracefully about the floor, partaking in conversations before their dance began. Wax candles in crystal chandeliers ran the length of the room and basked everyone in a forgiving light, giving the room an air of mystery.

"Would you care to dance, Charlotte?"

She smiled but shook her head. "You should dance with someone else. People will talk if you show too much inclination toward me."

He shrugged. "Let them talk."

At her raised brow, he growled and downed the last of his champagne before stepping away from her and moving about the room with casual elegance. Every step reminded her of a large cat searching for its next victim. Yet no one could be a victim when it came to Mason. Never had she known a better man than Lord Helsing. And after her marriage with James and meeting the friends he frequented the gambling dens with, she wondered if she could count on her fingers how many good men she knew, in truth.

Mason walked toward the card room and slipped out of Charlotte's sight lest she make him dance with a green country girl ripe for the picking. He looked about the room and spying his friend, George Lord Mountbatten playing piquet, joined him.

"Helsing," his friend said, clapping him on the shoulder. "Good to see you." George gestured to the gentleman sitting across from him. "You remember Sir Phillip Penry?"

Mason nodded and sat. "Of course," he said as he

watched George play for a moment before he won the hand with a flurry of excitement.

Sir Penry pushed back his chair and stood. "Well that's me done for the night. I'll leave you gentleman to it, shall I?"

George laughed and started to slide his winnings toward himself. "Come man, the night's still early. You never know, I may have a bad round and you could win all your blunt back."

"Lord Mountbatten have a bad round?" Sir Penry scoffed. "That is something I shall never see."

Mason laughed. "How many good men have you fleeced tonight, George?"

"A few," his oldest friend said, sitting back and lighting a cigar. "What brings you in here? Are you running away from the maiden debutantes that are nipping at every gentleman's heels hoping for a marriage proposal?"

The thought of Charlotte and her anything but debutantes nipping assailed Mason's mind and he shifted in his seat. "No. Not a debutante."

George whistled and leaned forward. "Who is she? Do I know her?"

Mason debated telling his most trusted friend for only a moment. George would never disclose his secret and bring censure down on Charlotte. "Lady Remmick," he said, without ceremony. George's shock was clearly visible before he composed himself with a gulp of brandy.

"She's married."

"I know," Mason said, stemming the urge to roll his eyes. "But..."

"What?"

"I want her. I think I've wanted her a lot longer than I would admit to even myself." Mason rubbed his jaw and met George's stunned gaze. It wasn't often he could confound his friend, but on this occasion he had.

"Lord Remmick will never let her go. He's not a man I'd wish to cross. You'd better be certain Lady Remmick is worth—"

"She is," he said, cutting him off. "You've seen the bastard. He whores around worse than the women walking the streets in Drury Lane. And it's only a matter of time before he kills Charlotte either by disease or force."

"He's violent?"

Mason nodded. "Yes. Often. Charlotte says he loses his temper over the simplest things and no matter what anyone says or does, there is no stopping his rage. He's unbalanced, to say the least."

"What are you going to do?" George asked, summoning a footman for more drinks.

"Charlotte wants to keep it a simple, secretive affair. But how can I let her go home and share her with that bastard?"

George shook his head and sighed. "You'll have to. Until Lady Remmick is ready to leave his lordship and face the fall from grace she undoubtedly will, you can do nothing. My advice is to enjoy your liaison. It's been too long since you've had one."

A shiver of unease rippled down Mason's back and looking over his shoulder, he spied Lord Remmick glaring at him from the gaming room door.

Mason turned back to George and swore. "The bastard's here."

"I noticed. And what's more, he's coming this way."

Mason braced himself for the forthcoming confrontation with his lordship. His skin crawled when Charlotte's husband slumped into the chair across from him and smirked.

"Gentlemen," Lord Remmick said, the smell of spirits and sex emanating off his breath and clothes.

Mason fought not to cringe. "Lord Remmick," he drawled. "To what do we owe the pleasure?"

"Come Lord Helsing. Or should I call you Mason, as my delightful whore of a wife does?"

Mason noted George visibly stiffened at the insult to Lady Remmick. Mason shrugged lest he clasp the bastard about the neck and strangle him. "You may call me whatever you choose. But call Lady Remmick, your wife should I remind you, a whore once more and I'll make sure you cannot speak another word for a week.

Lord Remmick grinned and pulled out a container of snuff. "You owe me."

Mason raised his brow. "What for?"

"For fucking my wife, of course. You should know there is nothing that Charlotte does that I do not know about. And last night she left our home and did not return until the early hours of this morning. The way you watch her, pant at her flesh like a dog in heat makes it easy for me to know it was you she visited."

"Really?" Mason took a sip of brandy and wondered who in Charlotte's household was spying on her. Not to mention the thought that she could possibly be beaten later tonight by this blight on society made his blood boil. "Prove it."

"Ah, but you see that I cannot do. Perhaps not this time at least. Even so, I want five-hundred pounds delivered to White's in my name by tomorrow lunch." Lord Remmick smirked. "And don't delay."

"I will not. Wherever Lady Remmick went last night it was not to me," Mason lied. "So you may keep your requests for funds to yourself. Perhaps you ought to ask Lady Remmick's herself for blunt if you're so short. She was the one, after all, who brought all the money back into your family name."

Charlotte's husband's face mottled red in anger. Mason relished the sight, wanting to strike at him in any way he could. But never would he disclose to this bastard what Charlotte and himself had done. He had made love to her, and no man, not even the pathetic specimen of manhood before him would mar his memory.

"Touch her again and I'll ruin you."

Mason laughed. "You'll ruin me? A man already ruined by his vices of hard living and drinking? Should you spread such vicious lies about London, you'll not only hurt Lady Remmick ,but yourself. Don't be a fool."

His lordship stood and clasped the table for support as he swayed. "Five hundred. Not a penny short," he said, before leaving.

Mason met George's worried visage and inwardly groaned.

"He knows."

"So it would seem," Mason said, thinking over what he could do and coming up blank. "He can't prove anything. And there is not an iota of a chance of me paying him a penny. I'll not let Lord Remmick make Charlotte into his prostitute."

"You'll have to be careful from now on," George said. "Lord Remmick will be watching her like a hawk now that he thinks he can gain funds from her nightly pursuits. And if that fails, he's likely to challenge you to a duel."

Mason drank down the last of his wine and pushed back his chair. "Lord Remmick will be lucky if I do not challenge him. And I will ensure that Charlotte's reputation is safe from scandal," he said, walking back toward the ballroom.

He found Charlotte standing beside Lady Furrow, her

puckered brow and pale countenance indicative of her recent encounter with her husband. Anger thrummed through Mason's body and an urge to come across Lord Remmick in a darkened ally had never sounded more desirable.

He bowed as he came to stand before them and smiled at Charlotte who didn't seem to be the jovial woman he'd left, not a half hour before. "Would you care for a stroll, Lady Remmick?" He kept his gaze on Charlotte and waited for her to decide. She bit her lip and something in his gut clenched. Married or not, he was attracted to this woman like his lungs were to air. The need to make her happy, to be with her in any way he could, was like a drug to his system. "Charlotte," he prompted.

She cast a nervous glance at Lady Furrow, then nodded. "Of course."

Mason took her hand and placed it on his arm before moving toward the French doors leading out toward a lawn patio, overlooking the garden.

"Your husband arrived and sought you out, I see," he said, as they walked toward the corner of Lord Wilson's townhouse.

"Yes. He was here." She paused. "He wanted to know if I enjoyed myself last night."

Mason shook his head at the scum's audacity to ask such a question to his wife, especially given the way Lord Remmick lived his own life. Yet, a prick of guilt stabbed at Mason that he was being selfish wanting to continue the affair with Charlotte. But then the memory of her beaten black and blue from her husband pushed away such guilt. Lord Remmick didn't deserve her. And Mason wanted her and would have her, at any cost.

"What did you say?"

"That I did. And then Amelia, Lady Furrow, obviously

noting my husband's furious countenance said we'd had a delightful time at her home playing cards." Charlotte smiled. "James didn't know what to say or do. He left shortly after."

They slipped around the corner and the smell of London, the distant sounds of the city, echoed across the sky. The yard this side of the house encompassed a small pavilion covered in a rose climber and neat garden beds set out in symmetrical shapes with lawn between the beds for ease of walking. Mason pulled Charlotte closer to his side and walked them toward the private pavilion. This side of the house was shadowed, moonlight their only means of light.

Walking into the circular structure Mason noted no chairs only the railings which looked out onto the foliage about them. Charlotte stopped and looked up at him expectantly. He slipped a lock of her hair behind her ear and ran a hand down her nape, electing a shiver to course through her body. His own hardened before he leaned forward and kissed her.

She met his eagerness with one that matched and his breath hitched in his lungs. The feel of her tongue twining and mimicking his had him as hard as a rock within moments.

He spun her about and pushed her against the railing, then slowly lifted her gown from behind. From here should anyone look, they would only see a couple taking in the garden around them and nothing more. Not a man who was about to take a woman up against a garden structure and enjoy every delicious, sensuous moment of it.

"Mason, what are you doing?" she asked, gasping when he slipped his finger to run around her stockinged thigh.

"Seducing you. I want you," he said feathering kisses

across the back of her neck. Charlotte didn't say anything, just pushed against his straining cock and Mason had his answer. He strained against his breeches and closed his eyes when her hand came behind and clasped him through the material.

Untying the frontfalls quickly, he lifted her skirt and stepped further between her legs. His cock strained for release yet the urge to tease Charlotte, make her want him as much as he did, made him rein in his baser needs.

He slipped a finger into her hot, wet passage and fought for control when she tightened about him. "You're so sweet, Charlotte," he said, kissing her neck while he kneaded her breast with his free hand. "I'm going to make you come."

"Yes." Charlotte rode his finger and undulated in his arms like a woman beyond thought. Mason removed his finger and stroked his phallus against her sex. She gasped and lifted her arms to clasp him about his nape.

"Please," she whispered, hardly audible.

"What, darling," he said, slipping a little inside of her before rubbing once more against her sex. "Tell me what you want."

"You." She tried to move and impale herself on his shaft and Mason bit down on a groan before continuing to tease them both senseless.

"I want you. All of you."

Unable to hold off any longer, Mason leaned Charlotte a little over the railing and slipped inside. Her hot core clasped tight about him and he felt a slight tremble course through her sex. "You're so close," he gasped, sheathing himself fully within her.

He held still for a moment and took a steadying breath less he spill himself before he'd brought her to orgasm. And then Charlotte shifted a little and started to ride him.

Mason's axis tilted. Never had he known a lady to act in such an erotic way before. He clasped her hips and guided her as she rode him from in front. His balls ached; in fact, his whole body ached for release. It was a heady experience indeed, being fucked by a woman in such a way. Yet not any woman, but Charlotte.

She made soft mewing sounds before her tempo changed, slowing down and riding his whole length. "You make me feel…"

"Let go, darling." Mason let her ride him and felt as the first contractions tightened about his shaft. She moaned into the cool night air and unable to stand the relentless torture of her orgasm that pulled at him, he joined her.

Lights blazed behind his eyelids as he emptied himself deep into her womb. "Charlotte," he said, gasping. "You're everything to me."

She let go of the railing and turned a little in his arms to look up at him. Her eyes shone bright in the moonlight and Mason hoped she could see from his own features just what she made him feel, what she was coming to mean to him.

"Am I?"

He lightly kissed her and pulled her hard against his chest. "Yes."

Her tentative smile warmed his blood. "I'm glad for I'd hate to be the only one here who feels this way."

Mason nodded. He knew exactly how she was feeling. Like a life was blossoming before them, like the roses climbing the pavilion in which they now stood. He would give her time to realize she had no future with Lord Remmick and then he would be there for her. But it would have to be her choice. Charlotte would face social ruin and – although an easy decision for him – Mason knew not so for a woman of class. But she would eventually leave the bastard. And when she did he'd be there to protect her. Marry her.

He kissed her again and let the embrace deepen into a firestorm of desire. In the interim, he'd ensure Lord Remmick and himself would have a little tête-à-tête.

Face to face.

In private.

Mason didn't have to wait long for his chance to talk to Lord Remmick. He stood in Drury Lane and watched as the bastard rutted like an animal with a whore from the streets. Her gasps of what sounded like pain making his lordship moan with pleasure.

The bastard was sick.

Mason waited for him to be finished then walked toward him, the whore walking quickly away and tying her gown as she did so.

"I hope I didn't make you rush, Lord Remmick."

His lordship started and looked up from tying his frontfalls. "You didn't rush me, as the night is only young and I've plenty more of those whores yet to fuck." Lord Remmick took a sniff of snuff. "What do you want, Helsing? Permission to screw my wife?" Like I said earlier tonight, pay me the money tomorrow and I'll gladly give you her cunt."

Helsing punched the bastard and a fire in his stomach ignited as he watched him smack against the cobbled road.

"I should kill you now. No one would know." Helsing leaned over Charlotte's husband and kicked him in the balls for good measure. "Start treating your wife with respect or I'll hunt you down each and every time I see a new bruise on her face and I'll make sure you sport one a lot bigger and darker." He paused. "Do you understand?"

Remmick glared and wiped the blood from his nose. "You're a fool to care for her. She's the coldest, most uncaring woman I know. And she's married to me. You can never have her."

Helsing refused to react to the bastard's taunt. Charlotte was anything but what her husband proclaimed her to be. Never had he known a more caring, warm person in all his life. Why, the day they'd met as children was entirely due to her finding his lost wolfhound. She had been a girl full of life and immense chatter in those days, and she would be again one day, as soon as Mason rid her of her diseased and unhinged husband of hers. Freed her of a life of which she was no longer happy to be a part.

"Do you understand?" Mason repeated, kicking Lord Remmick in the stomach just for the sake of it.

Remmick sputtered and rolled onto his side. "I understand, Helsing. Now fuck off."

Mason smiled. "Gladly. Goodnight."

He walked away and summoning a hackney, headed back to Mayfair. As the cab pulled away he looked out and saw Remmick get on his feet and stagger off into the night. Unease crept down his spine and he hoped he hadn't just made Charlotte's life harder. That had never been his intention.

CHAPTER 10

Charlotte walked into the foyer of her London home and watched as an array of luggage was piled at the base of the stairs by busy footmen. A moment later, her cousin, Rose from Bath walked serenely into the house and came toward her, a smile on her lips.

"Charlotte, it's so wonderful to see you again. You cannot believe how excited I am to be in the capital at last."

Charlotte kissed her cheek and noted her cousin's appearance and apparel. "And you, my dear." She looked toward the carriage and frowned when it pulled away from the curb. "Where is your mama? I thought she was to accompany you."

"She fell ill, unfortunately. Or perhaps, fortunately I should say. But that does not matter as I'm here now and you're married and able to chaperone me to all the balls and parties."

Charlotte started at this tidbit of information that she'd gone from having guests to stay to being a lady who sponsored a debutante about London. It was Rose's first

London season, due to Bath having been a disaster the year before. The poor girl had formed a tendre for a particular gentleman, who had hightailed off to London before asking Rose to marry him. Rose's mama, worrying about her daughter 's future, had suggested London. A change in location was surely what was needed, to raise her daughter's spirits. And so here she was.

"Well, I hope Aunt May recovers soon. And of course I'll chaperone you. In fact, you'd better have your things unpacked and perhaps have a lie down before tonight. We're attending a masquerade."

"I'm not sure if mama would approve of me attending a mask, Charlotte. Are they not where trysts of the night occur?"

Charlotte laughed and hoped that *was* the case. Especially when it involved Mason and herself. She shook away the unhelpful thought. "Not the masquerade we're going to, my dear. But I will not lie to you, there are sections of society that partake in such risqué behavior, but I'm not one of them." The image of what she'd done the night before in the garden bombarded her mind and heat coursed up her neck.

"Are you well, Charlotte. You seem to have reddened. You're not blushing, surely?"

Charlotte laughed, covering up her discomfiture. "I'm fine dearest. Now, run along upstairs, I'll have a maid sent up to help you unpack and prepare you for tonight."

"Thank you," Rose said, kissing Charlotte's cheek. "I'm so grateful to you. I'm sure by the end of the season I'll be happily married like you and living probably across the park from this very house."

"I hope so too," Charlotte said, pushing her cousin toward the stairs. "And make sure you rest. That's an order."

Rose smiled. "I promise."

Later that evening, Charlotte stood beside Rose in a room full of the ton, some dressed in dominos and masks that completely concealed their identity. Others, like herself, wore an elaborate hair piece or half mask and regular gowns. Either way, the room was a kaleidoscope of color and elegance. Charlotte smiled at Rose and wondered if she too had looked like that three years ago, full of hopes and dreams, when she'd had her debut in London.

The memory of James and his elegance of courtship that had been a mask like the one she now wore, made her tremble with regret. How had she not sensed his rotten core? Rose clasped her arm and pulled her from her musings and Charlotte promised she wouldn't let her cousin suffer the same fate. She would have her marry for love and nothing less.

"He is here," Rose said.

Charlotte frowned and turned to her cousin. "Who is here, dearest?"

"The gentleman I wrote to you about. You know, the one who had to leave on urgent business in London just, before he could propose."

Charlotte refrained from mentioning to her young cousin that the gentleman's hightailing it to the capital could have been because an offer of marriage was expected. It was just like something James would do. Take his fill and then walk away without a backward glance, and not a blot on his conscience.

"Perhaps you could introduce me." Charlotte smiled at Rose and she nodded her eyes bright with excitement.

"I would like that," Rose said.

Charlotte turned her attention back to the guests, some dancing, others gambling and chatting in groups about the room. She spied Amelia and waved to her dearest friend who was dressed as a tavern wench, her bust almost spilling from her gown.

Feeling a prickling of desire across her skin, Charlotte looked toward the card room and spied Mason leaning casually against the door. He was dressed in a black superfine suit and black silk breeches. His waistcoat embroidered with intricate gold stitching matched his golden cravat. Never had she thought she'd react to a man like she did when he was present. Like her skin, her very being was attached to him in some way, reliant on him to keep her alive. Alive with desire and love.

"He's coming this way."

Charlotte tore her gaze from Mason and turned toward Rose as a sliver of dread ran up her spine. "You never told me the gentleman's name, Rose. Who was it that you formed an understanding with in Bath?"

Rose leaned toward her to enable privacy. "Lord Helsing from Somerset. Perhaps you know him as I understand his country estate resides not far from your parents' home."

Charlotte fought the bout of nausea that settled in her stomach. "Lord Helsing was the one from whom you expected an offer of marriage?"

Rose nodded. "Yes. He courted me most ardently in Bath and mama was sure he was in love with me. But then he just up and left, made an excuse to papa about urgent business in the capital."

Urgent business. Was she, Charlotte, the urgent business? She had wondered why all of a sudden he was back in town and seemingly courting her. Anger thrummed through her veins at the thought he'd used her cousin and now her. But that wasn't really the case, as Charlotte was the one who sought him out. Asked him to lie with her.

She watched him walk toward her and noticed his step faltered when he spied Rose standing beside her. Charlotte ground her teeth. What Rose had said was true. He'd courted her cousin and left her hanging like a ripe apple on a tree.

He continued on and bowed when he stopped before them. Charlotte held his gaze before she curtsied. "Lord Helsing, you know my cousin, Miss Rose Lancer of course."

Charlotte didn't miss the widening of his eyes at the manner of her introduction that held no warmth.

"Of course," he bowed. "It's a pleasure to see you again, Miss Lancer."

"Rose, please, Lord Helsing. We are acquainted well enough for you to use my given name."

"Perhaps in Bath, my dear but in London it is best to use your proper salutation." Charlotte glared at Mason and hoped he could read the fury over his behavior in her eyes. "My cousin was telling me about your time in Bath, my lord."

He nodded his eyes narrowing in suspicion. "Would you care to dance, Miss Lancer. For old times' sake."

"I would love to, thank you, my lord."

Charlotte smiled at Rose and watched as he led her cousin onto the floor. They did make a striking pair. She was fair and he was not. Both tall, yet perfectly proportioned for one another. Not to mention the fact that neither were married.

Despair threatened to make her ill. What was she doing? Having an affair with a man who could not save her. Only she could save herself and as much as Charlotte hated to admit it, she was too weak to leave. To throw society the biggest scandal of the year and divorce James like she should. But she could not. And here she was, angry at Lord Helsing, and all because last season, he had courted her cousin in Bath. Perhaps.

Granted having done so, he should have offered marriage. But had he really courted her or was Rose's attachment to him so strong that she desperately hoped his attention toward her was just that?

Charlotte turned away from the couples dancing a fast quadrille and went to find the ladies' retiring room. She slipped through a door and walked toward a footman who stood before a door near the end of the passageway. Tiredness swamped her and all she wished to do was leave.

"Charlotte!"

She whirled to find Mason storming toward her, his countenance one of frustration and concern.

"Where are you going?"

"Away from you." She continued past the footman and toward a door that seemed to lead outside. He followed her and she fought the urge to turn about and scold him in front of a servant.

The balmy night air kissed her skin as they stepped onto a darkened terrace. Charlotte continued on and heard Mason close the door behind them.

"Charlotte, stop."

She did and took a moment to calm down before he joined her. "I request that you leave me be."

"Don't be absurd. Why would I do that?"

She shrugged. "Oh, I don't know. Perhaps because you owe my cousin a proposal of marriage after you courted her last season."

"I never courted her. I was her friend and acquaintance, but that's all." He frowned and ran a hand through his hair. "She resembled you and I suppose I gravitated toward her because of that."

Charlotte stepped away from him. "You used her then, which is worse. How could you, Mason?"

A muscle ticked at his temple. "I apologize if it seems like I did, but I didn't do it intentionally. You did marry someone else, Charlotte."

"You didn't ask me to marry you, Lord Helsing need I remind you?" She took a calming breath. "Why didn't you tell me about your relationship with her? Why keep it a secret?"

He tried to pull her into his arms, but Charlotte pushed him away. "Don't touch me. Tell me why you didn't say anything?"

"Because I knew you'd react this way. Innocent or not, my actions with your cousin seem heartless. It was not my intention."

The thought of Mason with Rose turned Charlotte's stomach and made her tremble with jealousy. "Did you kiss her?"

He paused. "No."

The quiver in his voice gave him away. "You lie." Charlotte clasped her stomach and swallowed. Hard. "How could you lead her on so, then come to London and seek me out as you did. Kiss me, make love to me?"

"When I realized her attachment to me was beyond that of a friend, I left. I suppose I panicked. I know I should have stayed and let her down in the nicest way possible, but I didn't. Men kiss debutantes all the time, Charlotte, not all the mamas make them marry."

Charlotte scoffed. "You're a cad and I'm a whore. What am I doing?"

She pushed him away again when he went to pull her into his arms. "What we're doing is wrong and we need to stop. I'm married and you need a wife at some point." She sighed and met his troubled gaze. "Just the thought of you and Rose together made me insanely jealous. I can't stand it. But I can't help it, don't you see? You may not marry her, but you will marry someone, and what we're doing is only going to make it harder for me to let you go."

"Then don't let me go. I have a younger brother, Charlotte. He can produce the heirs for my family."

She shook her head. "If only it were that easy." Charlotte walked up to him and kissed his cheek, taking the opportunity to breathe in his delicious scent of sandalwood and something else, something exotic, one last time. "I know you want what's best for me, but my marriage mistake is the burden I must bear. Please leave me alone and go on with your life. I really do wish you well."

He stepped away from her and immediately she felt the loss of his heat. A lifetime loomed ahead of her, cold and bereft of any love, children, and solace.

"I will do as you wish but only because you've asked this of me. But let this be known, Charlotte. I neither agree nor want to. This decision of yours is yet another mistake made by you."

She gasped. "How can you say that to me?"

"Because it is true." He strode back to the door and paused before opening it. "I love you," he said, before taking his leave.

Charlotte slumped against the balustrade and tried to push down the severing pain tearing through her chest. "I love you too," she whispered, to nothing but the warm night air.

. . .

Mason stormed through the guests at the masquerade and didn't bother hiding his thunderous gaze. He entered the card room and found George sitting alone while he watched others around him play cards. Mason slumped into a vacant chair and summoned a footman for a brandy.

"Problem?" George drawled, smirking.

Mason cursed. "One of my own making. Damn it." He took the glass offered to him and drank it down without pause. "Charlotte's… I think I've ruined everything."

"Really? What did you do?"

"Why is it," Mason said, summoning the footman for another drink, "that women jump to conclusions that are inaccurate and then, will refuse to hear what you have to say."

George laughed. "You're asking the wrong man. I have no idea."

Mason took a calming breath and sat back in his chair. The brandy helped to cool his ire but Charlotte's words stung. That he'd fallen in love with her didn't help. With any other lady he'd have walked away without a backward glance at such an accusation from a married woman. But with Charlotte he couldn't. He cared for her. Her opinion mattered to him. That she thought him a cad who used debutantes and moved on to married women at will hurt. He shook his head.

"Miss Lancer's in town," Mason said not looking at George. The last thing he needed to see was his best friend's knowing smile.

"I see."

"I'm not sure of Miss Lancer's exact words to Charlotte but I was accused of using Miss Lancer for my own amusement in Bath. She even asked me if I'd kissed the girl."

"Had you," George asked, taking a sip of his drink. "I always wondered."

Mason ground his teeth. "I wouldn't call it a kiss. We were at a ball and she was upset over something trivial. I strolled with her about the pump room before I kissed her hand on departing. The way Charlotte was speaking, anyone would have thought that I lifted Miss Lancer's skirts and taken her there and then."

George frowned. "You did seem to take to the girl more than any other in Bath. Even you knew her attachment to you was growing."

Mason ran a hand through his hair. "I know, damn it. And I should have been more circumspect in my interactions with her. I made a mistake."

"And one I doubt Lady Remmick would be willing to forgive. You need to apologize and speak to Miss Lancer. Tell her that you're sorry but your affections lay elsewhere. And then speak to Lady Remmick and grovel at her silk slippers until she's inclined to forgive you as well."

"When did you become so knowledgeable?" Mason said, meeting his friends gaze for the first time.

"It's not something I like people to know, unless the need arises from a close friend."

Mason laughed. "Thank you."

"Don't thank me yet. Your apology hasn't been forgiven," George said.

Mason cringed and wondered just how he was to win Charlotte back and gain her forgiveness for a sin he never actually committed.

CHAPTER 11

A week later, Charlotte sat a circular table at Lady Bates' garden party and tried to keep her attention on the conversation going on around her. Yet, no matter how much she tried, the fact that Lord Helsing was present and right at this moment deep in conversation with Rose at another table, made it impossible to do so.

"If you keep looking over at them, he'll know you're wondering what they're talking about."

Charlotte took a sip of tea and raised her brow at Amelia. "I am wondering what they're talking about." She sighed. "I know. There is no hope for me."

Amelia laughed. "Yes there is. But your fixation is creating a little attention. Although I do believe they think your staring is due to the fact Lord Helsing is only days away from proposing to the girl."

Charlotte clenched her jaw at the thought of Rose and Mason married. Not that she didn't wish the very best for her dearest cousin and his lordship was certainly that, but because her life would continue on as before. With bouts of serenity followed by episodes of fear.

She heard laugher and clinking glasses and spied James flirting with some elderly matrons of the ton. He could certainly charm the ladies when he wished too. Pity he couldn't control his anger as well.

"I wrote to my father yesterday about James."

Amelia clasped her hand and smiled. "I'm glad you did. What do you think he'll do?"

Charlotte shrugged. "I'm not sure he can do anything. James is the one who'll have to initiate a divorce by catching me with another man. He'll never do it even if he had found out about me and Lord Helsing."

"I'm so sorry, Charlotte. I wish I could help in some way."

She smiled. "You do help by listening when I need someone to talk to. Like now for instance," Charlotte paused. "I'm going to ask James to depart for our country estate. I know he'll probably say no but if he doesn't then I'm going to leave instead. I'll not let him hurt me anymore."

"Under the circumstances I think this is a wise decision for you." Amelia cleared her throat. "Rose is coming—"

Charlotte looked up and the breath in her lungs hitched at the sight of Mason standing beside her cousin. His masculinity all but oozed from his attire and his casual elegance made her ache in all the naughty places on her body. She shifted on her chair and refused to react to his knowing grin.

"Lady Remmick," he drawled, picking up her hand and kissing it lightly.

Charlotte felt her mouth open before she realized what she was doing and closed it again. "Lord Helsing," she managed to say without sounding breathless like she felt. "Are you enjoying the garden party?"

"I am. The temptations she has on offer this afternoon positively make my mouth water."

Charlotte heard Amelia giggle and heat suffused her face. "Yes the cakes are very nice." Mason smiled and she knew he was laughing at her. She narrowed her eyes.

"Is it alright if I go and speak to Jane Carter, Charlotte? She's just arrived."

Charlotte nodded to Rose but didn't take her eyes off Mason. "Of course." She started when Mason sat beside her. Again, she was tempted by his very essence and she cursed herself for being a woman without willpower.

"Please, take a seat." Sarcasm all but dripped from her tone.

Lord Helsing watched her, his gaze intense and a shiver ran down her spine. Charlotte absently heard Amelia excuse herself and before she could join her friend, she felt a finger slide against her knee.

Charlotte shut her eyes for a moment and reveled in the contact before she pushed his hand away. "Don't."

"When can I see you again?"

Tension coiled inside the pit of her stomach and she almost moaned at the thought of being with him just one more time. Of having his lips on hers. All over her, in fact.

"You are seeing me," she said, laughing to hide her unease.

Mason leaned toward her. "I want to hear your voice rasp against my ear as I make love to you," he said, his breath but a whisper against her cheek.

Charlotte turned her attention to the other guests and realized with dismay the ladies once sitting at her table were no longer there. Cursing and thanking them for the small tidbit of privacy she met Mason's burning gaze and shook her head. "No."

His finger ran along her arm and she shivered.

"Yes," he said. "There is a room two doors up from the conservatory. Meet me there in half an hour or so. Please, we need to talk."

Charlotte squeezed her legs together as the temptation to be with him made it hard to remain immune. Mason stood and left before strolling about the lawns, talking to other guests at the party.

She took note of where Rose was and smiled as she watched a young gentleman amicably talk to her, his hands gesturing wildly with some tale.

Should she join him? The temptation to do so was beyond anything she'd ever known before. And Mason knew it. He knew what to say and do to her to make her crave him; want him, as desperately as she sensed he wanted her. And what did he have to say?

Seductive fiend.

Charlotte stood and noted Lord Helsing watching her from across the lawn. She walked over to Amelia and let her know where she was going before heading toward the house. Excitement thrummed through her veins and a smile quirked her lips. Poor, Mason. After she'd finished with him today, he'd never try and seduce her before the ton. Never again.

Mason watched Charlotte casually stroll toward Lady Bates' grand London home and his body tightened painfully. The unconscious sway of her hips pounded his blood directly to his groin and all he wished to do was clasp her delicate body hard against his and have her in any way possible.

He took note of Lord Remmick's whereabouts and noted with distaste the gentleman's attempt at flattery and polite behavior. The bastard didn't know the meaning of either word and he doubted if he ever would.

Mason walked toward a footman and taking a glass of champagne started to stroll toward the house. He entered off the terrace and headed toward the conservatory. The house was quiet and inside one could barely hear the party taking place out on the lawns.

Walking past the conservatory the smell of exotic plants and fruits wafted across his senses before he entered the room further on that he sought. Charlotte lounged on a chaise longue, her elegance of ease sending a frisson of uncertainty to course through him.

"Lord Helsing." She smiled and his gut clenched.

"My lady," he replied, snipping the lock on the door behind him.

"I would like to get a few things clear before we go any further. What is about to happen between us does not change what I said to you a week past at Lord Wilson's ball. Our liaison must end and you must marry. Is that understood?"

Mason ground his teeth but nodded. "I understand that as long as you know I'll always care for you. I also wish to clear up your confusion about Miss Lancer. I never seduced or kissed her. I always acted with the most gentlemanly behavior around your cousin. Today I apologized not having realized that she'd read more into our association than I had intended. She has forgiven me."

"Really?" She smiled and his gut clenched. "You never kissed her?"

"No," he replied walking toward her. "It's not Miss Lancer I want."

Charlotte held up her hand and he stopped. "I'd like to try something that I saw in a book once. You must allow me my way or I won't forgive you either."

Mason grinned. "What do you wish to do to me, my lady?" All sorts of erotic thoughts began racing through his mind.

"Come and sit on the day bed."

Mason did as she bid and watched as Charlotte knelt before him. The breath in his lungs hitched when she slid her hand up his thigh, his body wholly focused on what she was doing.

"I've been fascinated ever since I overheard some women talking as to whether a man could be pleasured in such a way. I searched out some books of James' and it seems to be true." She unclasped his frontfalls and Mason shifted in his seat. He moaned when she ran a finger down his length. "It is true, my lady," he managed.

"I enjoy your tongue against me. Love how wantonly you make me feel when I'm against your mouth."

"I'm more than willing to show you again, my dear." And he would if she'd allow it. Nothing in this world would please him more than to make Charlotte happy. He stilled when she kissed the end of his cock, her sweet, tongue tasting the very essence of him.

"It's my turn to make you moan, my lord."

Mason clenched his jaw, lest he follow through on his urge to thrust between her sweet lips. Dear God, how was he to get through this exquisite torture she had concocted for him. A quick learner, she licked down his length then took him wholly into her mouth. Heat and the lightest suction made his balls ache. "Charlotte."

She threw him a wicked smile and then continued her ministrations. Mason shut his eyes and prayed he had the stamina to last longer than he thought possible at this point. Her innocent loving of his member, her sweet sighs and moans as she tasted and enjoyed her attention to him near unmanned him.

Tension coiled inside as she relentlessly took his full length. Her goal to make him come, unfortunately all too close. "Charlotte, come away. You'll make me—"

"I want you to." She glided her hand up and down his length and he swallowed. Hard. "In my mouth. I want to taste you."

Mason watched as she continued to love him. He wanted to run his hands into her hair, hold her against him and fuck her mouth, but he could not. Instead, he saved the fantasy for another time and alternatively grabbed the daybed for support.

Lights blazed behind his eyelids as he came. His balls ached and never had an orgasm flowed throughout his body sending shivers of pleasure that consumed him. Charlotte moaned and kissed his member, making sure to lick the last drops of his essence before she sat back. "Did I please, my lord?"

Mason pulled her up on his lap and took her lips in a searing kiss. He let her know through his embrace, what she made him feel. What he would continue to feel for her if only she would let him. "Just knowing you're in this world pleases me, Charlotte. Everything else is a boon."

She laughed, the sound more carefree than he'd ever heard before and his heart thumped loud in his chest. "I meant what I said the other night, Charlotte."

She met his gaze, her own visage becoming serious at his tone. "What was that?"

Mason pushed a lock of hair from her brow. "That I love you."

Charlotte nodded, her eyes overly bright. "I know."

CHAPTER 12

Two days later, Charlotte sat in the library of her London home and waited for James to wake up. He lay, sprawled on the settee before the unlit hearth, his clothing askew and an empty flask of liquor lying uncorked on the floor.

She thought about throwing a vase of water on his head, before common sense halted her actions. The conversation she was about to have with her husband would be bad enough. She didn't have to make it any worse.

When the lunch gong sounded, James stirred. She absently watched him wake up, his shaking hands and sickly demeanor no way resembling the man she had married. "When you're able I wish to speak to you, my lord."

He started at her voice and looked over the settee's back. "What do you want?" James rubbed his jaw and yawned. "Your lover owes me five-hundred pounds. Make sure he pays up."

Charlotte stemmed her urge to throw the blotter on

James' desk at his head. Instead she remained calm, and waited for him to join her. He heaved himself up from the lounge only to sprawl into his desk chair a moment later. Nerves churned in her stomach over the coming conversation.

"I want you to leave," she said, her voice stronger than she felt. "I have informed my father of your treatment of me and my desire to separate from you. You will leave this house today, or I will."

James threw his head back and laughed. Charlotte glared. "I mean what I say James. I'll no longer allow myself to be treated with unkindness and violence."

"You stupid whore. I'm not going anywhere and neither are you." He stood and Charlotte lifted her chin, refusing to give way to her fear of him. James came around the desk and leaned casually against its side, watching her silently.

"But then, I suppose I could divorce you and have you publicly shunned and termed a adulterer. It would certainly make our acquaintances happy knowing I'd be rid of the common trash I so wrongly married."

"Common or not I saved your estate with my money. You're a liar and a fraud. You give off this persona as someone loving, kind and charismatic when it pleases you and yet you're capable of the cruelest touch and words that I've ever known."

James shrugged, seeming not to care of his downfalls. "A divorce would ruin your sister's chances of a good marriage."

"Louise is old enough to look after herself. And over the last few months I've come to realize that if the gentleman who wishes to marry her would cry off because of my indiscretions as you call them, then he is not for her. I want my sister to marry for love and nothing less." Charlotte sat back and felt, deep inside her soul, that what she stated was true. Louise would never wish for her to continue living this type of life. A life that was no life at all.

For all her father's wish for his children to marry high into the peerage, his children themselves were never inclined to aspire to those great heights. And Louise would probably marry a local boy from the sphere in which they circulated in Somerset and be happier with her choice than any town dandy with status and great connections.

"So honorable," he scoffed. "And when we're divorced will you run off to your lover, Lord Helsing? Beg his lordship to marry you and try and redeem some sliver of your reputation."

"I have no immediate plans other than to move on with my life," she said without censure. "Now I asked you before and I'll ask you again. Which one of us is leaving? You or me?"

"Neither. Now get out. The sound of your voice droning on makes my head hurt."

Charlotte stood. "Good bye, James."

He clasped her arm, his grip painful, biting into her skin like tiny daggers. "Do not attempt anything foolish, Charlotte or you'll pay dearly for it."

"I've already paid dearly for my foolish action by marrying you. I've paid for it every, single day for the last two years." Charlotte wrenched her arm free and walked out the room. She chastised herself for the fear she felt whenever she was around him. It was like walking on cracked ice.

She heard James bellow for the carriage as she headed toward her bedroom. Charlotte rang for her maid and started to place the items she wished to take with her on her bed. Having received word from her father that he'd support her whatever decision she made, she began to prepare her departure to Grillon's Hotel.

Charlotte ignored her maid's shocked countenance when she told her of her plans, and instead thought over what she would do with her life away from James. Of course, if he chose to divorce her, she'd be ruined, but so would he be. She'd not allow him to come out of the trial in the House of Lords smelling of roses. No, Charlotte would ensure all his misdemeanors behind closed doors were aired along with any he could name against her.

When James sobered up and thought on his threat of divorce, he'd soon change his mind. No matter how much he hated her, or regretted their marriage, he wouldn't want anyone to know what type of man he was. It would seem she would have a separation but no divorce. Which would suffice, she mused, taking a watercolor painting down from the wall and placing it in a trunk. As long as she didn't have to live under the same roof as her abusive husband, her life would be much brighter. She was sure of it.

※

Later that day, Charlotte checked in at Grillon's and followed a footman to the second floor and her suite of rooms. The hotel in Albemarle Street had everything she'd hoped for, a drawing room for guests, a private bathing suite and a more than generous bedroom. Her maid had a small room adjoining the drawing room to enable her privacy.

Charlotte wrote a quick missive to Amelia, notifying her of her change of circumstances and contemplated informing Lord Helsing. She should probably let him know, and yet, somehow it seemed wrong to run to him as soon as she'd left her spouse. It was silly of her to think that way, but then, Mason couldn't marry her, so she should hold true to her wish for him marrying someone else. There were many women in London who'd suit him and could create a loving home he so deserved. And with her out of his life, he'd be free to pursue such a future.

Giving the missive to her maid to take downstairs, Charlotte looked about her new home and for the first time in an age, felt content. A feeling she could get used to, she was sure. Dinner arrived at seven and just as Charlotte was about to sit down at her small dining table, a knock sounded on her door.

Moments later, Amelia strolled into her suite, dressed in a high waisted green silk gown, her visage one of merriment. No doubt, Charlotte mused due, to her change in circumstance.

"I came as soon as I heard your news." Amelia joined her at table and nodded for some wine. "Lord Remmick would not leave, I gather?"

"He refused and threatened me not to do anything stupid." Charlotte paused. "It was time I stood up for myself and so I left."

"Does he know?"

A shiver raced down Charlotte's spine imagining how angry James would become when he found her gone. The poor staff would brunt most of his ire before he'd think to look for her. Not that she hoped he would. "Not yet," she said.

Amelia frowned and played with a diamond necklace about her neck. "You think he'll seek revenge in some way or make you return to him?"

Charlotte stood, no longer feeling hungry. "Of course he will. He'll probably demand I return home. But I won't, not under any circumstance. He can have my money and my reputation. I don't care anymore. Since being with

Lord Helsing, I've remembered what it is like to be alive again. How to love and be loved. I can never go back to James."

"You're in love with Lord Helsing."

It wasn't a question and Charlotte started at her friend's disclosure. "I am." And she was, more than anything in the world. Just the thought of Mason made her smile, her body heat and her heart sing. He was her everything and because he was so, she had to let him go. "But it doesn't matter as James will never divorce me and therefore my feelings for Mason are of no consequence. There is no future for us. He must marry and beget an heir. Something, that if you haven't noticed I've been unable to do for my husband.

"When it comes to Lord Remmick I cannot find fault for your inability to bear children, Charlotte." Amelia paused. "It is possible that the problem to have children lies with Lord Remmick and not you at all, dearest."

"Perhaps," Charlotte said, yet her two miscarriages which she'd told no one about made the problem seem all the more hers than anyone else. She pushed the distressing memory aside and sat on a chaise lounge. "I've told Lord Helsing he has to leave me alone and marry someone else. Thankfully, Rose has moved her attentions elsewhere, which I'm happy about."

"Where is Rose?" Amelia said, looking about the room.

"Aunt May arrived yesterday and they've gone to stay with her sister in law on Jermyn Street. I thought it only right to let my family know of my change of circumstance and Aunt May thought it best if Rose was distanced from me."

Amelia gasped and clasped her hand. "I'm so sorry, Charlotte. They do not understand what it would be like to live in such a distressing marital circumstance. I'm proud of you for leaving Lord Remmick. And as you know, Lord Furrow and I will always be ready to help you should you need anything."

Charlotte nodded and pulled her best friend into a hug. "I know and I thank you."

Amelia laughed. "You're very welcome."

CHAPTER 13

It took a week for James to locate her. Charlotte stepped from Grillon's Hotel and breathed in the warm spring air before turning left and heading down Piccadilly. Her father had sent her some funds a few days ago and finally she was wholly independent from her husband.

The only blemish on her happiness was that Lord Helsing had not tried to seek her out either. And although Amelia had said he'd asked after her health at engagements she attended, Charlotte, did not understand why he never just asked outright where she was.

The memory of the lovemaking assailed her and along with it came excitement tinged with hurt. Did he not care or had he decided that her decree for him to marry another was right and had decided to act on it? What a silly fool she'd been. And yet...

"Charlotte!"

She stopped and looked across the street and spied James weaving his way through the local traffic. Anger all but thrummed along every line of his body and fear curdled in her stomach. Charlotte looked around, noted the many people about, and took some solace in the fact he wouldn't dare touch her on a public street.

Yet, his furious glare could prove her wrong.

"You will return to whatever hovel you're living, pack your things and return home immediately. How dare you make me a laughing matter for the ton of London?"

"Married couples live apart all the time. Our circumstances need not be any different." Charlotte lowered her voice. "And I will not return home, not under any circumstances."

"You bloody well will," he said, his tone laced with menace.

"I will not."

Out of nowhere, James hit her with his small walking cane. Charlotte put up her arm to fend off another strike when he raised his arm once more, yet the cane never came back down. She looked up and watched with awe as Mason broke the cane over her husband's back and threw him against a shop wall.

Never had Mason wanted to kill a man as much as he wished to kill Lord Remmick right at this moment. Having seen Charlotte on the street, he'd watched her stroll along the shop windows, her ease and happiness not something he'd seen glowing from her eyes since being back in London. But that had all changed the moment her brutal husband had seen her and taken her in hand. Literally.

He squeezed the filthy mongrel's throat and relished his fight for air. "If I ever see you come within an inch of Lady Remmick again I'll kill you. Do I make myself clear?" Mason released his windpipe a fraction so he could answer.

"She's my wife," Lord Remmick managed to gasp.

"Not anymore. From this day forward she isn't. Don't look for her and don't ever think that I don't know people who could make your disappearance seem like an accident," Mason said through clenched teeth. "Do I make myself clear?"

Lord Remmick tried to push him away and the urge to make the bastard pay assailed him. He stepped back a fraction then slammed his fist into his lordships gut before doing the same against his jaw. Charlotte's husband's head snapped back and hit the brick wall behind him before he slumped to the ground, unconscious."

Mason turned to Charlotte and pulled her back toward her hotel. "Are you all right?" he asked, trying to gauge her mood.

"I am, thank you." She stopped walking and Mason turned to her, wondering what she was thinking. She cast a quick look toward her husband and he noted her slight shiver. He wanted to pull her into his arms and show her that he'd never allow anything to happen to her. Neither by Lord Remmick's hand nor by anyone else's. If only she'd let him.

"Thank you Mason." Tears welling in her beautiful blue orbs. "You're my knight in shining armor."

"Always, Charlotte. Surely you know that by now," he said.

She nodded. "Did you mean what you said back there? That you'll protect me forever?"

"Yes. I know you think there is no future for us but you're wrong. As I said before, my brother is more than capable of keeping the family name and property in our rightful hands. I'm old enough to decide what I would like to do in my life. And that is to be with you. Come away with me. We'll move to the continent or New York. Start a new life where no one knows us."

She bit her lip and Mason felt like his heart would pump right out of his chest. Never had a reply mattered as much as Charlotte's did now.

"Yes. I'll go with you. Wherever you wish, just as long as we're together."

Mason smiled. "I love you Charlotte King."

Charlotte leant toward him and wrapped her arms about his neck. "I love you too," she said, kissing him.

Mason allowed the embrace to deepen and cared not a fig what anyone watching thought or said about their actions. From tonight, they would be on board the fastest ship to wherever they decided to go and London and its tonnish ideals – no one could ever live up to – could well and truly go to the devil.

EPILOGUE

Two Years Later – New York

Charlotte threw the letter she'd received from her father, which had been accompanied by one from her late husband's solicitors and realized that she felt nothing but relief.

Mason walked into her parlor carrying their one month old daughter and a love so true filled her heart. True to his word, Mason had kept her safe and out of Lord Remmick's clutches and by doing so, they'd lived a life she'd never thought possible. Mason passed Lily to her and Charlotte kissed her beautiful little girl's pudding cheeks.

"What did the letter say," he asked, shuffling through the pages.

"Lord Remmick is dead. Was killed in some alley in East London. The solicitor wasn't very forthcoming in details but I'm sure you can imagine what happened."

Mason shook his head and came to sit beside her. "So I suppose we'll have to make you a lady again?"

Charlotte threw him a puzzled frown, wondering what he was talking about. "Excuse me?"

"Now that you're a widow, perhaps you'd prefer to be named a bride instead?"

Charlotte clasped his stubbled jaw and smiled. "Are you by any chance asking me to marry you, Lord Helsing?"

Mason took Lily onto his knee and turned their daughter to face Charlotte. "What do you think, Lily? Should Mama agree to marry Papa do you think?"

Charlotte laughed and kissed him quickly. "Of course I'll marry you. I love you."

"I love you more."

She shook her head, knowing such a thing could not be possible, but they could argue about that later. In bed. *Tonight.*

A CAPTAIN'S ORDER

Scandalous London, Book 2

※

Lady Eloise Bartholomew's trip to Australia on the shirttails of her adventurous brother ends in tragedy when he dies from a fever. But with the conventions of English society suspended on the high seas, she finds passion and excitement in the arms of a rugged ship's captain—only to be dumped back into the ton, still burning from the fire ignited in her and the loss of the only man she could ever loved.

More at home on his ship than dallying with the ton, Gabriel Lyons, now the Duke of Dale, intended never to set foot in London again. But when an elder brother dies, and the woman who claimed his heart over his love for the ocean brings him home, he knows he has to face the secrets of his past. He can only pray their love will survive the scandal that sent him away, the lies he has told her, and the duel he must fight for his honor and her hand.

CHAPTER 1

Colony of New South Wales, 1810.

Eloise sponged her brother's brow and still he twisted and turned with a fever that wouldn't abate. The doctor she'd summoned the night before, after Andrew had fallen ill at dinner, called it a fever brought on from an insect bite.

She swallowed hard and refused to believe the statistic he'd dealt her. All those he'd nursed had died. It wasn't fathomable. "Andrew, try and drink a little." She lifted his head and he moaned an awful sound that reeked of death.

Her vision of him blurred. She couldn't lose her brother. Not so young. Not here. He should be home raising hell in the ballrooms of the ton, not dying an awful death half way around the world with little or no amenities to help him.

"Fetch the doctor again. He's getting worse." Eloise managed to get a little moisture between his lips before he started to shake uncontrollably. His face was red, blotchy with heat, and yet he moaned he was cold.

She prayed to god that should this be his end that it would come quickly. A good, kind soul didn't deserve to die in such heinous conditions. "Andrew darling, talk to me. Tell me what to do."

He didn't answer, his breathing ragged then laboured. Panic clawed at her throat that he wouldn't see another sunrise. Oh dear god, she couldn't be left alone. He was all she had left. "Please, dearest. Please try."

The bedroom door slammed open and Dr Jones walked briskly to her brother's side. He checked him over, his heart, listened to his breathing, noted his eyes and stood back, a consoling, pitying face she didn't want to see.

"I'm sorry Lady Eloise, but your brother will not make it. He's showing all the signs that I have noted before with this disease. We will try and keep him as comfortable for as long as possible, but you must prepare yourself."

A blackness threatened to consume her. "Prepare myself? Are you delusional! I don't care what you have to do, but you can't let my brother die. Now search through that bag of yours you carry about and pull out a miracle."

He patted her hand that lay over Andrew's brow. "I'm not being intentionally cruel, my lady. Your brother is dying. I'm sorry."

She shook her head not wanting to acknowledge the truth of the words. And unfortunately, Andrew did pass and her brother was no longer.

A few hours later, Eloise sat beneath the veranda of the Governor of New South Wales' home in Sydney town wondering how she'd come to be an orphan. Because that was, exactly what she was now. A woman of independent means in the most awful of ways.

She would have to return home to England and soon.

A CAPTAIN'S ORDER

The trip she'd looked forward to with her brother was no longer viable or wanted. This country was hard, hot and somewhere she'd always associate with grief.

Yes. It was definitely time to go home.

"Captain. Please, I will pay double for the fare back to England, or however far you can take me."

The man looked at her as if she were daft. And maybe she was. Her voice certainly had an desperate edge even she cringed at hearing.

"We're full. You'll need to find another vessel." He turned his back on her and started to shout out orders to his men.

"The ship I sailed here on left last week. There isn't another one for months and I must return home. I have no family left here. I'll sleep on deck if I have to, just give me passage. Please, I'm begging you."

He sighed and ran a hand through his hair. His stance one of annoyance. He turned and took in her appearance. "Fine, but you'll pay double and the only place for you to sleep is in a small closet that runs beside my room. I doubt sleeping in with the crew would be wise." He nodded toward her luggage. "Are they your bags?"

"Yes. I didn't bring a lot as I thought to have clothing made here to suit the climate. And well…"

He held up his hands. "Spare me the details. Come aboard." He yelled out to one of his crewmen who jogged over to them. "Take…ahh." He gestured toward her. "I'm sorry, I don't know your name."

"Oh, of course I should have said. I apologize. I'm Lady Eloise Bartholomew."

The captain raised his brow and a pained expression crossed his features. "Take Lady Bartholomew to my cabin and clear out the stores room beside my room, put a cot in there for her. And Hamish, make sure the crew know she's off limits."

Eloise felt her eyes widen at the captain's words. *Off limits.* What did that mean? Had she inadvertently placed herself in more danger here than on the mainland with animals and insects that could kill you within hours? "Thank you," she said as she followed the other man. The captain walked off without another word and busied himself on deck, obviously busy with getting the ship ready for sail.

She wished she were returning home on better circumstances, but she was not. Only after a few weeks of arriving here, she was about to embark on another six month journey across the seas.

She groaned. How would she ever bear it...

CHAPTER 2

Six months later off the coast of England, 1811.

The sea ebbed and flowed around her; great waves rolled and brought her ever closer to home. Yet never had Eloise felt more homeless.

England.

So different from the dry, barren, and barely civilized colony of New South Wales. Six months it had taken them to travel there, on a brother's whim to visit new climes and enjoy his newly acquired inheritance. An inheritance now solely hers because of his sudden death to a fever they blamed on a mosquito.

Eloise shook her head at the knowledge such an insignificant bug could kill a man in his prime. A much-loved brother left on foreign shores many miles from where he, the earl, should have been laid to rest at Belmont House, Surrey.

They docked not an hour later in the murky brown

water of the Thames. The filthy stench from the overpopulated waterway made her yearn for the crystal streams that surrounded Sydney Town.

"Right this way, m'lady, if you please." No doubt, years of wind and sea had hardened the gravelly voice of the man stepping around her.

Eloise followed the hunched gentleman off the boat and walked toward a highly polished, enclosed carriage. Dark and foreboding, it reeked of her future.

That of a lady. With a title she no longer deserved . . . .

Because the daughter of an earl did not yearn for the touch of a hardened sea captain. Nor desire, nor crave, his roughened, stubble-strewn jaw marring the skin of her most intimate places.

And yet she did. Desperately.

Before she was three feet from the vehicle, the door opened with a snap, and a childhood friend, now woman, alighted—ribbons and frills flying about her like a kite in strong winds—pulling Eloise from her troubled thoughts.

She laughed. "Emma." She hugged her dearest friend, the overpowering smell of rosewater making her eyes water. "I have missed you."

"You are home. Oh, dearest, England has been such a bore without you. How have you been? You must tell me of your voyage and all you know of this wild land you have visited. I long to travel and would visit such a place if my Bertie would allow. But"—Emma rubbed the distinctive lump under her skirt—"because of my current condition I am not allowed."

Eloise smiled, biting back the nip of jealousy over her friend's happy news. "Congratulations. I'm happy for you and Lord Rine. And as soon as I'm home and settled, I promise to tell you all."

Well, perhaps not all. How could she explain the Lady

Eloise Bartholomew had fallen in love? Lain with a man out of wedlock and enjoyed every decadent, sinful moment of it.

Deep in her belly, a thread of desire thrummed at the thought of his hands. His lips, grazing her skin, kissing her breasts, her—

"Are you well, Eloise? You look flushed." Emma frowned. "Oh dear, I do hope you are not falling ill, my dear."

"I'm perfectly well, I—"

"I heard of Andrew's demise." Emma clasped her hand. "I'm so sorry, dearest, truly sorry. He was a wonderful man, whose life was cut tragically short. I wish I had been there for you."

Eloise blinked, refusing to give in to emotions already running high. "Thank you. I wish you had been there as well."

"Come," Emma said. "Let's get you home."

Eloise settled her skirts on the leather squabs, the excess material feeling bulky and awkward around her legs. For months, while on the ship home, she had worn breeches, shirts, and a jacket to keep her modest when in the view of the captain's crew. The freedom had been liberating for a girl used to the strictures of society. After the death of her brother, something inside her snapped.

No longer was she willing to pass through life unhappy, doing what everyone else thought was right. For, within a moment of time, one's life could be over. And she'd lived by the rule for six months. But her hiatus of freedom had now ended. She was an aristocrat, and with such dire circumstances came the dreaded high-waisted gowns of English fashion, and responsibilities she now had to face.

"Tell me," she said, changing the subject. "Everything I

have missed while I was away. What's the latest on dit scandalising the ton?"

Eloise listened to her friend's gossip and exploits covering the last fifteen months, but sadly, she had heard it all before. Life, it seemed, did not change in London during the season or at the ton's country homes during the winter. As usual, life here was tedious to the extreme.

And the complete opposite of what she had tasted.

CHAPTER 3

Somewhere between the colony of New South Wales and England, 1810.

Gabe sat on a wooden water barrel and watched as Eloise tried to learn the art of tying knots with his second in command, Hamish Doherty. He laughed to himself at the irony of the situation. For the last two month's that's exactly what she'd been doing to him. Tying him in knots.

With a will of their own, his eyes took in her summery gown, the gentle breeze giving him a view of her lovely ankles every now and then. Her attire wasn't appropriate for this type of voyage and he really ought to supply her with some breeches and shirts.

He swallowed as the vision of what she'd look like in such attire flooded his mind like a rogue wave. All her delicious curves would be there for him to admire. The roundness of her bottom, a lovely handful he'd ache to clasp.

The thinness of her waist accentuated by breasts that were lovely and pert.

Oh dear lord. He was turning into a perverted fiend.

Eloise laughed at something Hamish said and a twinge of jealousy shot through him. He stood and walked over to them before picking up his own slip of rope and sitting.

Hamish nodded and stood. "I have things to do, Lady Eloise. I'll leave you with the good captain to carry on our lesson."

"Thank you, Hamish."

She didn't meet his eye, only seemed to concentrate more on the knot she was learning.

"Do you need some help?"

Eloise pulled the rope from her hand, a muffled curse escaping from her lips. "It's supposed to be a stopper knot. I can't seem to thread the rope right."

Gabe moved to sit beside her and took her hand. Her skin was soft, warm and made his flesh sizzle with desire. He felt the rate of his heart increase at the close proximity to her. Taking a deep breath, he rallied himself to calm down. It was only a knot after all.

"You must with this knot hold your hand solidly in this way. The rope will then thread and link more easily for you. Here," he said, picking up his discarded rope. "Let me show you."

He quickly finished and held it out for her to review. She smiled, laughing he mused at her own inability before trying again. Again he helped her to ensure her hand remained solidly fixed in one position and with a couple of tries she pulled the stopper knot into the form it should be.

"I did it!" She stood and waved it at Hamish now manning the wheel. "Look Hamish. The knot."

He nodded. "Well done, my lady. I knew Captain Lyons would teach you well."

"Thank you." She sat, staring at him and again he was left breathless at the innocent beauty of her features. No rouge sullied her complexion; she was as natural as the elements around them. Perhaps even more beautiful. "I've never accomplished anything like that before. My hobbies are usually limited to needle work or drawing."

"Both amiable qualities, but out here, it's always helpful to have other skills." He pulled her to stand and started to walk toward his cabin. "Talking of practicability, your attire is probably not the most comfortable on board a ship like mine. I hope you don't think me impertinent, but maybe you'd like to wear breeches and shirts instead of gowns. I think I have some clothing packed away that would fit you."

Her emerald eyes sparkled like gems in the sun. "That would be wonderful. I would love that."

He led her downstairs to his cabin and bade her welcome to his room. He'd been steadfast in keeping her out of this space. Just the thought of what they could do together, enjoy together in a bed that mocked him almost physically hurt.

It was easy throwing a few clothing items together and if he looked rushed it was because he was. The sooner she left the better.

"These should fit. You can change in here if you like and come up on deck."

She walked up to him and took the clothing from his hands. Eloise caught his gaze and a question lurked beneath her long eyelashes and one he ached she'd ask. "Why have you never tried to kiss me, Captain Lyons? I've caught you watching me and yet you never even once try and see if your desire is reciprocated."

Gabe leaned against the dresser with an air of nonchalance that was a total farce. "Do many men try and kiss you, Lady Eloise?"

"Just Eloise, please. I think our circumstances and location warrant the loosening of society's rules." She grinned. "As to your question I will not deny that I've been approached on more than one occasion for a stolen moment or two."

"Really." He tried to shake the building anger that other men had tasted her lips. Clasped her delectable body against theirs and taken her mouth in an embrace that would beckon them for more forever. "Are you so in demand?"

She shrugged. "I am an Earl's daughter and now that my brother's gone it is time I secured my future and married."

Sadness flickered through her gaze and Gabe wanted nothing but to go to her, pull her against himself and hold her. "Is that what you really want?" Something told him it wasn't. To ask such a forward question as to why he hadn't kissed her only meant one thing. Maybe she wanted him too.

Gabe closed the space between them and looked down, waited for her to meet his gaze. His body thrummed with suppressed desire. Every impulse in his body wanted to devour, take, conquer and enjoy, but he couldn't. "Have you ever been really kissed, my lady? Kissed to within an inch of your sanity, like your body is burning and needing the person in your arms as much as the air you breathe?"

She licked her lips and he bit back a groan. "I've never been kissed like that."

"I want to kiss you like that."

Eloise nodded, her eyes wide with wonder. "You do?"

"Oh yes, I most certainly do." And he did. No sooner had the words left his body did his mouth fuse with hers.

Never had he felt such soft lips. Lips that copied each of his movements like a mirror image. Gabe swept his tongue across hers as he pulled her hard against his chest.

She fit him like a perfectly made kid leather glove. Her breasts pressed against his body and through her gown he could feel her nipples bead with desire. Her breathing hitched as he plundered her mouth, sank deeper and pulled her further into the world he desperately wanted her to seek.

He wanted her. His cock strained against his pants and, rogue ship captain that he was, he ground himself against her sex. She gasped, her eyes going wide at the unfamiliar touch, but still she didn't pull away. Instead, her arms came about his neck as she lifted herself to fit against him more snugly.

Gabe groaned and continued to kiss her. Without heed, or support they stood in the centre of his cabin, locked within each other's arms, their mouths locked in an endless battle of need.

Eloise gasped and he knew what their bodies were doing to one another was making her hot, exciting her and bringing her closer to release. He could make her come fully clothed and the thought itself was enough to confirm his plans.

He ran his hand over her bottom and clasped her high on her leg, lifting her and placing her directly against his heat. Her fingers clenched his hair as a slight blush rose on her cheeks.

She was close, so tantalizing close, but not there yet. He supposed he could lay her over his desk, throw up her skirts and lick her to fulfilment. But not yet, he doubted she would be ready to go that far…yet.

Instead he made certain her sex was being teased in exactly the right location. Over and over again he fucked her little bud with his cock, teasing her, making her want more.

Eloise didn't disappoint. "Yes. Oh yes." Her breathy words sent fire to his groin just as she hugged him as her orgasm took hold. Gabe continued to dry fuck her as the last of her shuddering subsided. His cock ached for release and he shook away his need.

There was plenty of months left on this ship left yet.

He took her lips in a quick kiss. "Do you like my kisses?" He grinned.

"Your kisses are exemplary, and they have more than satisfied me, Captain Lyons."

He pushed a lock of hair from her face and marvelled at her beauty. "I always strive to keep my passengers happy. A captain's duty."

She laughed. "And a passengers fortune."

CHAPTER 4

London, 1811.

Eloise stood in a gilded ballroom in the home of her dearest friend. The surprise celebration marked her return to England and to society. But the crush, intoxicating smells, and the deafening volume of the entertainment overwhelmed her senses.

Although she pasted on a smile, nodded, and spoke at the appropriate times, her heart was no longer in this life. The satins and jewels held no interest. The men in their finely cut suits did not stir her desire nor engender thoughts of futures together.

Nothing.

Only one man sat in her thoughts, and yet, he should not. For had she not left him in Africa? His home. Or so he had told her when he refused to travel the rest of the distance to England to be with her.

Marry her.

"Darling, there is someone who wishes to meet you." Emma dragged her toward the opposite end of the room. "He's very handsome and just perfect for you."

Eloise bit back a resigned sigh. She should move on with her life, find a husband to take care of her. Love her, just as she'd planned. "Emma, I do not wish . . . that is to say—" She paused when the gentleman in question came into view. Oh dear, he was handsome if one could ignore the excessively starched shirt collar he sported. Eloise curtsied and allowed Lord Rine to introduce her to Lord Daniel Fenshaw, a baron from Norfolk.

The gentleman looked to be in his early thirties if the smile lines about his eyes were any indication. With an athletic build, he towered over her, and made her modest height seem small and delicate. But something in his eyes gave her pause and tempered her response to his ardent words and charm.

"I understand you have recently arrived back from the colonies. The land, I hear, if one could live without niceties, is quite beautiful."

"Yes, it is," Eloise said. "Although I didn't venture to the bush, I did see many beautiful sights. The plants and their flowers are unlike any I've known, and the creeks and rivers run with the clearest water I've ever seen."

"Sounds like you miss it."

She paused and wondered if such a notion was true. "I was not there long as my brother fell ill only a week or so after arriving. I don't miss anything of the country other than my brother who is buried there." Perhaps that wasn't quite true. The freedom she'd enjoyed there would forever make the strictures of this life fray her patience. Her trip home had been just as wonderful and enjoyable. Not to mention . . . pleasurable.

The captain.

A man whom she watched, awestruck, when he climbed the tall masts and rigging. Steered the pitching ship through choppy waters determined to capture the vessel for itself and submerge it in a watery grave. Only after two months she was pleased to call him her friend and often times her only confidant. She'd hidden her growing lust for him until, unable to stand the situation any longer, she'd taken a chance and seduced him…

The day in their cabin when he'd first made her orgasm, fully clothed and in the middle of the day would be a memory she'd cherish forever.

Eloise snatched a glass of champagne from a passing waiter. "The country will forever hold a place in my memories, but I doubt I will see it again. Dreadfully long voyage, you understand." She smiled as she met Lord Fenshaw's gaze, hoping her blasé tone would end the conversation.

"Yes, Lady Rine mentioned you travelled back via a merchant ship to Africa, then caught the Oriental from there." He paused and smiled to a passing acquaintance. "What was the name of the boat you travelled to Africa on, if you recall?"

Eloise frowned, and a tingle of unease prickled her skin. "Ah, I believe the ship was called Esperance, my lord."

He nodded but said nothing; instead, he looked out over the throng of guests milling around them. Eloise searched for Emma, meaning to slip away and join her, when his lordship turned to her with an intense, probing stare. She shifted her feet, unease creeping down her spine from the awkward silence that settled like a dark cloud over them.

"Six months is a long time for a lady to be at sea. Alone." The gentleman cleared his throat as if thinking better of what he was about to say. "I was saddened to hear of your brother's death. He was an honourable man."

Eloise looked down at her drink and blinked, refusing to give way to more tears, a most inappropriate reaction, which came upon her when people spoke of Andrew. "Thank you, my lord. That is very kind."

"Are you attending the masquerade ball at Lord Durham's on Saturday?"

A smile quirked her lips when she noted Emma making her way across the room to her. "I am. 'Tis an event I've been told not to miss."

He smiled in response. "It's an event I would not want you to miss, Lady Eloise." Holding her gaze, he bowed before taking his leave. Eloise watched him go, and the unease that prickled her skin before now stabbed. She turned to Emma, wondering why his smile had not reached his eyes. Insincere, as if he knew something she did not.

Not yet at least.

CHAPTER 5

"So, dearest, what do you think of Lord Fenshaw? Isn't he the most fabulous man?"

"Oh, very much so." Eloise fought the urge to roll her eyes at her friend's absurd notion. "From memory, his sister came out the same year we did. Has she married?"

Emma's face clouded with sadness, and she wondered at it. "Yes, Miss Fenshaw. A beautiful woman, if not a little flighty and rebellious."

"There is nothing wrong with a woman wanting independence." Eloise regretted the sharp edge to her tone as soon as she'd said it. She sighed. "I apologise, I did not mean to snap."

Emma clasped her arm. "Independence is all very well, but at what price? I believe Miss Fenshaw paid dearly for hers."

Eloise met her friend's gaze. "What do you mean?"

They walked toward the supper room and away from the crowded ballroom. "I do not know all the particulars, but what I do know is her brother, unable to control her bizarre and promiscuous behaviour, institutionalised the woman. You see, she kept running away. From what I know, she died three years ago in childbirth at the hospital. Rumour would lead you to believe Miss Fenshaw also tried to harm herself while living there. A terrible sickness the family couldn't cure with love and help." Emma paused. "Lord Fenshaw loved her dearly and was understandably devastated by the loss of his sister. But the exact, underlying cause of her demise and condition has never been known."

"How do you know this?" Eloise asked.

Emma leaned in closer to her. "I should not. No one should. Lord Fenshaw's family tried to hush up the fact his sister was a lunatic, but . . . servants do talk."

"Oh, how dreadful for them all, and poor Miss Fenshaw, she seemed such a lively and popular girl." Eloise sat at a table for two and welcomed the footman who brought over a fresh glass of champagne. Looking at her friend's morose visage, she set about changing the subject. "What are you wearing to the Masquerade?"

"I thought I should go as a Venetian courtesan. Bertie wishes to go as himself. Such a bore, don't you agree?"

Eloise laughed. "Not a bore, just being himself, I suppose. I'm not sure what I wish to go as." She shrugged. "I'll think of something."

"Well," Emma said, biting into a crab cake, leaving a little amount of dipping sauce on her chin. "You will want to think fast. The ball of the season is only two days away."

Eloise motioned to her friend's chin, then laughed when Emma's complexion turned as red as the lobster shell she now held.

. . .

A CAPTAIN'S ORDER

Gabriel Lyons, more formally known as, His Grace the Duke of Dale, narrowed his eyes at the buildings and magnificent townhouses gracing his square in Mayfair. For the tenth time that day, he wondered if he should call out to his midshipmen and order them back to the docks. Back to his ship and back to Africa. Return to a home, which, no matter how geographically distant, would always be a more welcoming sight than the one before him. To think, he, the Duke of Dale, chased the skirts of a recalcitrant Lady Eloise Bartholomew hundreds of miles, was an illogical notion. Yet, when his carriage pulled before his stately Georgian mansion, and his door opened, within a moment, he knew such a thing was indeed true.

Fool.

Gabe looked up with loathing at the Corinthian columns gracing his front door and inwardly cursed at his elder brother's inability to stay alive. With heavy feet wanting to drag him back to the docks, he walked up the steps. Always a man to allow his wilder side little-to-no restraint, Gabe despised the fact he needed to pick up the title of duke—and all the obligations and strictures with that title. The mere thought did not sit well with his restless soul.

A soul that yearned for the swell of the ocean, the smooth wood of the ships wheel, and sails billowing with the gift of wind on an endless ocean. Sand beneath his feet with every new and unexplored destination, many of which he had still to venture. And perhaps now, never would.

Gabe sighed. Here he was about to cause one of the biggest upsets in the ton in years with his return and his proposal to a woman who'd tamed his heart.

To a point.

He walked into his library and slumped behind his desk, clean of papers. Gabe made a mental note to thank his steward, who looked after all his estates in his absence. Laying his head back, he stared up at the ornate ceiling depicting cherubs and women, lying on silks, surrounded by fruit and flowers of every kind, and he thought of Eloise.

Their parting had not gone well...

The ship had sailed toward Cape Town, where the mountains behind the city peeked over the waves on the horizon. Gabe handed back the looking glass to Hamish Doherty, his midshipman, aware a part of him wished he could delay their landing. But he could not. The men were restless for the pleasures only land could afford. Women, and the services they provided, food, and a bed that did not sway were paramount in their minds. He could not delay any longer.

His lips quirked when feminine arms came about his waist, followed by a warm, lithe body against his back. Gabe clasped her hands and pulled her tighter against him. "Awake already? Did I not wear you out sufficiently enough last night?"

A chuckle against his back, followed by a kiss, fired blood directly to his groin. "I feel so alive and invigorated. I couldn't possibly sleep a moment longer. Even if the temptation to sleep in your bed is so very great."

Gabe turned and pulled her against him, allowed his hand to flex the globe of her arse. "Perhaps we should go below decks."

Eloise's lips took his, and once more, he was lost. Lost at sea in the arms of a woman whose innocence he had seductively taken. He savoured the delectable lips and met her thrust of tongue with his own, pulled away only when she started to rub against him like a purring cat.

"You do realise we are being watched," he said.

She stilled in his arms and looked over her shoulder. Gabe laughed at the unladylike curse from her lips. It seemed he was a bad influence on her.

"Perhaps it would be best, Captain, if we went below. I do believe I am in further need of your services."

"Is that an order?" he asked, pulling her toward the stairway, ignoring the catcalls following their every step.

"Yes."

Gabe stepped off the last step in the corridor below. At the saucy look she threw him, he lost his equanimity. He pushed her against the wooden wall and took her lips in a punishing kiss. Allowed his hard and ready body to undulate against her, brought a whimper to her lips that fuelled his raw need to take her.

Eloise lifted one leg and wrapped it against his hip, her hot core burning him through her breeches. Gabe released a hungry growl and clasped her delicate thigh, cursing her attire and wishing she wore a skirt for easier access. A quicker fuck.

Still, there were other ways around the predicament.

He slipped his hands from her and caught the buttons keeping him at bay. Every one popped and sprinkled to the floor; he ignored her startled gasp and knowing smile and shoved her pants down.

"No undergarments. A woman after my own heart." His heart thumped as he devoured the delicious, rumpled sight she made— rosy cheeks, eyes glazed, and body bare from the waist down.

"After your heart, Captain? I already own it."

Gabe met her eyes and took her lips in a searing kiss, welcomed her frantic fingers against his breeches, shivered when she pushed them down his hips and clasped his arse.

She was a wanton. His wanton.

Beyond caring where they were, Gabe lifted her and moaned when his rod slid easily into her wet heat. Eloise's hot core clasped tight about him as he pumped into her, the slap of the waves against the boat and the slap of skin all he could hear.

Her tight passage pulled at him in ways he'd never thought possible. Eloise had a beautiful soul, one he should have left alone, yet she tempted like a siren, a goddess of the sea, and he had not been able to walk away from the fire she ignited in him.

He'd wanted her from the first. And had taken her when the opportunity had arisen, the day Eloise had asked him to make love to her. The memory shot blood to his groin.

Like now, begging for him not to stop, and Gabe, unable to deny her anything, followed her command. The creamy, soft skin smelling of lavender intoxicated his senses.

And he was lost…

She threw back her head and moaned as their bodies continued to mate with a frenzied need. Heedless of their location he pumped into her relentlessly, wanting to feel her body clamp tight about him, quiver up his shaft and pull him into his own orgasmic pleasure.

"Yes. Like that."

He adjusted his hold to pull her legs higher about his waist. She gasped and he knew she was close. Little mewling sounds puffed out with each expelled breath and then she came. He kissed the scream from her lips, dragged her sensual tongue into his mouth and kissed her until his own release followed. Fuck this woman had him in knots. She held him captive and it suited him more than he'd ever admit.

"Your Grace, dinner is served."

Gabe opened his eyes with a careless nonchalance he did not feel. Inside, his body burned for her. Needed her, like a Clipper needed water to sail the high seas.

"Thank you." He watched the elderly retainer, in service since his father's time, hobble from the room. He adjusted his rod, hard and beyond uncomfortable, in his pants and wondered where Eloise was at this moment.

At a ball? Dancing? With another man...

He stood and walked toward the dining room, determined to have a quick bite and some after-dinner entertainment. Entertainment that would include his future bride.

CHAPTER 6

Eloise stood at the terrace doors and looked over the sea of unrecognisable heads at the masquerade ball. The ton had gone to extreme costs dressing up as courtesans, pirates, Venetians, gods and monks.

A smile quirked her lips when a man dressed as a wolf stalked his prey, the woman not at all fazed by such pursuit but indifferent and even a little annoyed. She sighed and watched Lord Rine and Emma waltz around the floor. They made a beautiful couple, obviously, very much in love.

Eloise beat down the loneliness she had come to accept these past weeks. It wasn't her fault Gabe had pushed her away. She had spoken up and asked for what she wanted. Him. His refusal was of his own choosing and nothing more she could have said or done would have changed his mind. A man not used to the strictures of having a woman about and what that would mean for his bachelor life.

Pigheaded captain. She adjusted her black mask to sit correctly on her nose, wishing to remain anonymous. The only part of her face people could see were her lips, painted a deep red this eve, the opposite of the natural look she normally sported when at balls and parties. Dressed as Galatea, a goddess of the sea, Eloise felt seductive and beautiful for the first time in an age. Emma had sewn a small dolphin for her to hold, and the gown she wore poured over her like water and looked just as transparent in some light.

Not that she expected anyone to guess who she was. But tonight was for fun, and she was determined to have some. She needed to keep her mind off a certain man who haunted her every dream and every waking hour.

Gabe.

"May I have this dance?" The rich baritone ran through her and left her short of breath. She looked at the man bowing before her and frowned. There was something…

The dark hair behind his full-face mask gave him away, not to mention the eyes, deep pools of blue that spoke of sinful nights and weeks of longing.

But it couldn't be. He was in Cape Town. Thousands of miles away.

"Gabe?"

He pulled her into his arms and swung her into the throng of dancers. "Ah, so my goddess of the sea knows who I am."

Eloise's knees threatened to collapse, and as if he sensed her shock, he placed his hand about her back and held her fast. The hint of ocean emanated from him, dragging her under a wave of feelings only the blackguard before her could raise. A man who'd allowed her to sail into the sunset without so much as a by-your-leave. And yet, when he looked at her like he was now, with hungry eyes and lips lifted in a sensual smirk that made her stomach clench, it was so very hard to stay angry at him.

She cleared her throat. "I'm amazed a ship captain would know mythological history?"

His lips quirked, and so too did her pulse. "I'm well versed in many things." The seductive glint in his eyes left her with no misunderstanding of his meaning, and Eloise ignored the desire that shot through her at being so close to him again. Ignored his thighs as they grazed against her skirts, reminding her of the fact he had allowed her to leave. Perhaps marry another. She looked over his shoulder, the pain of his abandonment a torment still.

Had he even cared for her at all? They had made love so many times that eventually she lost count. Was she only used for his satisfaction, a plaything to while away the many months at sea? He'd always been honest as to where he called home, and eventually they had docked in Cape Town, but what had happened next had been something she'd never even contemplated.

At first the chance to see an unknown land lifted her spirits higher than they already soared…until Gabe had explained he would not be accompanying her to England. Would in fact, be staying in Africa for the foreseeable future. Without her.

Just the memory made the bottom of her soul drop to the floor with a thump, as if an anchor had been heaved at her, splitting her heart in two.

"Hard to forget the man who left me." She quickly met his gaze, her own narrowing. "What are you doing here? I did not think you cared for England or anyone who lived there."

The arms about her waist pulled her closer than she should allow, and her body, remembering every decadent thing they had ever done, purred silently with the contact.

"You left me if I recall correctly. You must know I

could never forget you." His breath whispered against her ear sent shivers of desire along her spine.

Eloise moaned and allowed her hand about his waist to venture under his domino, allowed him to see what his touch did to her. Fired her blood and made her crave a secluded corner so they could be alone.

Then in a voice that belied her actions, she said, "Oh, but did you not say the last time we spoke, you would rather die than step foot in the cesspit they call England. That, and I quote, 'not even my delectable rump would change your mind'."

She quirked an eyebrow at the resounding chuckle.

"Forgive me, my lady, I was not myself. The thought of you leaving…well, shall we just say I did not take it well."

Eloise snorted. "You couldn't wait to be rid of me. After everything we had been through you couldn't even bother to see me off. Do not stand here and spout foolish words you do not mean." She stepped back and curtsied. "Have a pleasant evening, Captain. Oh, and a pleasant life, preferably one back in the Africa you are so fond of."

Considering the fury she noted behind his mask at her words, Eloise was surprised she made the corridor running adjacent to the ballroom before a large, voyage-roughened hand clasped her arm and pulled her to a stop.

"You know I never meant anything I said that day. I was upset. You were leaving me. Refused"—he pointed a finger at her nose—"to stay and live with me away from this life you once loved."

"Still love," she said, knowing she had never spoken such an untruth in her life.

Eloise noted the muscle in his jaw work while he digested her falsehood. Fear, unlike any she had ever known, assailed her when he let go and stood back, his eyes devoid of any emotion. "Forgive me. It seems I have been mistaken. I will leave you now. Goodnight."

A moment of panic left her stunned. She didn't want him to leave, just to punish him a little for leaving her broken hearted. Foolish bounder.

"You step back into that ballroom, Gabe, and you will never step a foot near me again."

A smile quirked his lips, which he smoothed before turning to face the wicked woman he loved more than any foreign country, ship, or the abundant wealth he had inherited. "Is that a threat?"

She turned and walked up the corridor before opening a door and disappearing into a room. Gabe looked along the passage and, noting its desertion, followed. Snipped the lock shut when he entered, and leant against the cool, wooden door at his back.

"You wished to say something, my lady?" He fought the urge to smile at her upturned, defiant little chin. He bit his lip lest he close the distance between them and nip at it until she begged for forgiveness or more. He'd take either.

"What are you doing here? How did you get an invite?"

"Ah." Gabe sat on a nearby chair and met her curious stare. "I was invited." "Really." Her mocking gaze indicated she did not believe his words for the truth they were. "You are saying, Captain Lyons, Lord Durham invited a terror of the seas, a man who has fleeced many an English ship, to his ball?"

He shrugged. "I did not fleece. It was always paid work. But your answer is yes."

"Why?"

Gabe looked at the signet ring on his left hand, the

Duke of Dale's emblem clear to see in the flickering candlelight. "Because it would not be wise to slight me."

"A sea captain? I always knew you were full of your own self-importance, but really, you are taking your charms too far."

He chuckled. "'Tis true. As a captain I would not be allowed entry, but as the Duke of Dale, there are few in society who would not invite me to their entertainment. In fact, bar you, I believe there would be none."

Gabe allowed the silence to stretch, watched an array of emotions cross Eloise's face. Shock, disbelief, acceptance, and finally anger. He stifled a sigh when the last annoying little sentiment came to the fore.

"You are the long lost Duke of Dale?" She paused, her mouth agape. "What?"

"Is it so hard to comprehend?" Certainly, his mannerisms and polite conversation had at times told of impeccable breeding and upbringing. Had Eloise never once wondered where he came from? What his life was like before the ocean became his home? "I came into the title just over a year ago. My brother loved his horseflesh and ultimately lost his life during a hunt last autumn." He sighed. "You see, I never wanted the title or this life. Only something very special could bring me back to England. Something—" He paused, gaining her eye. "Something other than family duty."

"You're a gentleman?"

The revulsion on her features stabbed at his gut like a knife. "And you're a lady. What's that got to do with anything?"

Curls bounced against her slender shoulders with her rapid head shake of denial. "Men have the liberty to live vicariously and freewill. Women do not. I think you know better than any, I am no lady…not anymore."

"You are my lady, Eloise." Gabe allowed his annoyance to tinge his tone. What was she saying? Because he had lain with her, loved her as any man would have, given the chance, she was no longer acceptable to him?

"A duke cannot marry his whore."

Taking a deep breath, Gabe clasped her hands. "You were my lover, but I never thought of you as my whore." He frowned at her indifference. "Eloise, if I believed you to be someone I could toss aside and forget about, would I be before you now, fighting for your hand and heart."

With a dubious look that stated she was not yet convinced, she pulled from his clasp, walked across the room, and sat. Her forehead crinkled in thought. "Did I not hear something about your abrupt departure from England?"

Probably, he mused. Most of London had. "Something like...?" he asked, not ready to tell her of his sordid past that spanned ocean and land.

"I cannot recall at this very moment, but I'm sure I will." She shook her head. "Does not signify, in any event. You owe me an apology."

"For?"

"Lying to me." She stood and came to stand before him. "A captain? Who turns out to be a duke? Why didn't you tell me?"

Gabe stood and pulled her into his arms. "If you knew who I was, would you have seduced me as you did? If I recall, the knowledge I was a lowborn whelp was a boon for a woman wanting to enjoy and learn the pleasures only a man could give. I doubt you would have allowed me to even kiss you had you known who I was."

Eloise hesitated, clearly fighting her desire for him, before she caught the lapels of his coat. "Even a lowborn whelp was able to capture the heart of a lady. I have missed you."

He lightly brushed her lips with his, inwardly smiled when she moved to deepen the kiss. "And I, you." With every moment, since the day she left, a part of him had been missing. He now realised what it was. His heart.

Gabe lifted her and carried her to a settee—not the widest of seats, but it would suit their needs perfectly well. Eloise lay before him and undulated against his chest. The silk gown splayed about her like a halo of sinful delight. The sensuous ploy made all the blood in his body dive to his nether regions.

Again.

Eloise watched Gabe strip off his mask and reveal the handsome face she had grown to love. His eyes swirled like the high seas in a storm when she sat up and helped him remove his domino, allowed her fingers to graze down his chest before stopping at his waist.

"You are not forgiven yet, Gabe."

"No?" He stripped off his shirt and absently threw it on the floor. "Tell me what I must do to please, my lady."

Unable to deny herself, Eloise ran her hand along the taut lines of his chest. Felt every sun-bronzed muscle with wanton abandonment. She swallowed when her gaze noted the hard ridge in his pants, and her own sex thrummed for him to take her there. Touch her. Take her back to the high seas and the many days of decadent love making they enjoyed.

Leaning up, she kissed his chest, allowed her lips to graze one pebbled nipple before tweaking it with her tongue. He tasted so good. Salty like the ocean but mingled with his own sweet flavour. She'd forever savour the taste.

Gabe clasped her neck, holding her against him. She nipped his skin, untied the front-falls of his skin-tight breeches, and watched mesmerized as his straining rod sprung free. His intake of breath made her stomach clench in desire. Eloise met his gaze while she stroked him, let her finger graze the tip and wipe away a drop of his seed as her palm slid over his member and stroked with just the right amount of pressure.

"Have you missed me?" She wrapped one arm about his muscular rear end and pulled him to his knees.

His eyes burned down at her, his ragged breaths all the answer she needed. She bent and licked his essence from the red, swollen head and welcomed the salty tang that settled in her mouth.

"Suck it." Gabe begged, his voice thick with strain.

Eloise slipped her lips over the velvety skin and did as he asked. Using her tongue, she teased every inch of him, sucked and pleased him until they were both rapidly breathing.

"You taste like sin." Eloise flexed her fingers around his taut balls, tight and sitting high against his body. She pulled away slowly, kept eye contact with him, until her lips finally slipped from his manhood.

He came down over her then, his hands frantic against her skirts. Warm air met her sensitised skin when he gathered the material to pool about her waist. He rubbed against her wet folds and mercilessly teased her. She shivered enjoying every moment of time together.

"Gabe," she panted, her nails flexing against the damp muscles covering his back. "What else are you going to do?"

"You want me?" He kissed the sensitive skin beneath her ear and pulled the neck of her gown beneath one breast. Her nipple, exposed to the cool night air, puckered and chilled. Eloise gasped and ran her hands through his silky strands, held him against her as his tongue laved, and his teeth nibbled her breast. She rubbed against him, tempting him to take her. Put her out of this misery. Still, he refused, merely slowed his movements, and tortured her even more.

"Yes, I want you."

He lifted her legs and situated them higher on his waist. "Have you missed me then, my sweet?"

"Yes." She moaned when the tip of his shaft entered her. She bit her lip, her need for him to take her unlike anything she had ever known. Her body felt aflame, her core tingling with the knowledge of what was to come. If only he would hurry. "Please, Gabe."

His eyes darkened before he pushed fully into her, making them one and whole. Eloise sighed against the exquisite sensation of having him in her once again. How could she have thought to live without such pleasure? Live without the man she loved, high or lowborn. She loved him and no one else.

Would no longer live without him.

He rocked into her, the cushions of the settee a comfortable buffer against the hard lines and rock hard man above. With every stroke, he touched the most special part of her soul that sang to him. Called and begged him never to stop.

Eloise flexed her hips, needing him deeper. Harder.

"Do what you just did, again," he gasped, the breath whispering against her ear.

She obeyed, and his rocking turned frantic, brought her all the closer to the pinnacle she climbed. The slap of skin and the smell of sex filled the room. Heedless of their moans and gasps, they made love with a reckless abandon. Gabe's lips remained hard and just as demanding as his rod that slid within her. Eloise cried out and clutched at him, afraid she might shatter entirely, like a mirror dropped from an astounding height. Pleasure thrummed through every muscle, every sinew of her body, left her breathless and boneless as they came.

"Marry me."

Eloise clasped his jaw and met his eyes. "Is that a captain's order?"

"No." He chuckled. "A duke's command."

CHAPTER 7

After taking some time to recover, Eloise and Gabe straightened their clothing and tidied each other up as best they could in a room with neither mirror nor refreshment.

"You have not answered my question, Eloise?"

The steely tone brought Eloise out of her muddled thoughts of what gown she would wear on her wedding day. Where they would live and venture on their honeymoon. She arched a brow at his vacant look. "Really? I thought I had." She walked toward the door and tried to keep the smile from her lips.

A hand clasped about her arm and pulled her around. "No, you did not. And I require one before we leave this room."

She raised her brows at his commanding tone. "Well, even though you lied to me about who you were, left me to sail from Africa to England all alone, and did not have the decency to call on me when you did return to London, I suppose I will."

"I may not have called on you, but I did seek you out as

soon as I could. You should know that if ever I was in the same county as you, I'd never be far from your side."

Her insides melted like Gunter's ices at the heartfelt declaration. Gabe kissed her and fire ignited in her soul. Eloise knew that with one word from her, she could make the wicked thoughts spinning through her mind a reality within moments.

My, she'd turned into a wanton. Not five minutes ago, they had made love with more passion than she had ever thought possible, and here she was once more, thinking of him naked, erect and loving her with his body.

Eloise met Gabe's hungry eyes and knew that with one word from her, she could make her wicked thoughts a reality.

She spied a chair beside the door and pushed Gabe into it. His grin gave away where her gesture had taken his thoughts. With them. On the chair. Having sex. Again. Eloise ran a finger across his shoulder, his superfine coat so different to the tattered, wind roughened shirts he wore at sea. "I don't want to return to the ball yet."

"Neither do I." He pulled her onto his lap and she straddled his legs, lifting her skirts out of the way, as she did so.

Again, the need to have him consumed her. She ripped at his front falls, his cock, hard and heavy in her hand. She came down on him quickly, their lovemaking taking on a whole new dimension. One of urgency that left them both desperate to find fulfilment only the other could bring.

Gabe groaned as she rode him fast, her core clamping down on him, leaving her aroused, and sitting on the crest to ecstasy. "Eloise, how I've missed you. Missed us." His deep baritone vibrated to her core and she climaxed. Cried out as wave after wave of pleasure shot through her body.

Gabe's clasp tightened about her hips, his fingers pinching her skin as he too came a second time.

Her body hummed in sated rapture. With Gabe back in London, the boring life of a lady now seemed far less dull. And she wasn't just any lady, soon she would be Gabe's lady sanctioned by the act of marriage.

She smiled. "I've missed you as well. Dreadfully so."

"I am very glad to hear it," he said.

Gabe kissed her before helping her to stand. Her legs felt wobbly after their interludes and she laughed at their escapades. "Does our betrothal mean you're going to living here in England from now on?"

He nodded. "Yes, but with one stipulation."

"And that is," she asked.

"I would wish we visit Africa at least once a year. Given time, I know you'll love where I made my home, and our children will love the golden sandy beaches that run for miles. I would like to show you all of that."

She had loved what she'd seen of Africa, short as it was. And what Gabe was asking was not at all a great deal of trouble. In fact, yearly holidays sounded perfect. "Perhaps through the English winter months."

He smiled and hugged her to him. "Sounds perfect." He kissed her, seemingly sealing the bargain on their future.

A ruckus from the ballroom brought Eloise back to reality. "We had better return to the ball. The midnight unveiling will happen very soon." Gabe retied her mask and opened the door.

"Good evening, Your Grace."

. . .

Gabe looked at the man who stood at the door, and a shiver of unease prickled his skin from the cold, calculating tone.

"Lord Fenshaw, to what do I owe the pleasure?" He walked into the corridor, pulling Eloise along and not allowing her the opportunity to speak or curtsy to the gentleman.

"No pleasure, sir, for I believe you have already had more than enough pleasure for one night." Fenshaw turned toward Eloise and bowed. "Lady Eloise."

Gabe beat back the urge to box the imprudent baron behind the ears. A bright flush swamped Eloise's neck, and Gabe squeezed her hand in unvoiced support.

"Was there something you wished to discuss?" Gabe raised his brows and waited for the words he knew would spill from the gentleman's mouth.

"Of course." Fenshaw paused and smiled at Eloise, a gesture more like a sneer. "I wonder if the woman you have ruined has any idea what a rake and bounder you actually are."

Eloise met his eye but said nothing.

"Rake and bounder no more, Fenshaw," Gabe said.

"Really?" He lifted his chin and looked down his nose. "I beg to differ. In fact, I would lay my entire fortune on the line Lady Eloise would dearly love to hear why I believe this to be true."

"I have no quarrel with you. Now, if you'll excuse us." Gabe took a steadying breath and walked away, knew as soon as he heard Fenshaw's mocking laughter that the man was determined to expose him. Perhaps even forever ruin what he and Eloise had come to feel. He paused and turned back, bringing Eloise to a halt by his side.

"Did you know, Lady Eloise, your esteemed duke

ruined my sister?" Fenshaw paused and strolled to a nearby painting, seemed to take a great interest in the family drawing hanging on the wall.

Eloise met Gabe's eye, then turned to face his nemesis. "Lord Fenshaw, perhaps you ought to speak to His Grace at some other time. Whatever your disagreement, Lord Durham's home is not the place to air such arguments."

"Oh, I disagree. I believe right here and now will do very well." Fenshaw smirked. "Your esteemed duke raped my sister, threw—"

"The sex was consensual. I never raped her." Unable to look at Eloise for fear of her reactions to the man's words, Gabe kept his attention on Fenshaw. True or not, the scandal had near ruined him years ago; no matter, he had not known…

"Threw her out," Fenshaw said. "Without a reference to her name, even when her belly swelled with his babe."

"She was our maid, Eloise, and she came to me. For weeks I pushed her advances away, but eventually I succumbed."

Eloise wrenched her hand from his and stepped away. "Miss Fenshaw was your maid? How is this so?"

He swallowed the dread that rose in his throat and threatened to choke him. "I didn't know she was Fenshaw's sister. And I never forced her. Please believe me."

"Is what this man says true?" Eloise asked, her face stricken. "Did you sleep with your servant and get her pregnant?"

Gabe tried to take her hand again with little luck. "I did, but please, let me explain the full truth."

"Who are you?" She shook her head. "I don't know what to believe."

"He is a bastard and one I have been longing to settle with." Fenshaw stepped toward him and stopped a foot from his face. Eye to eye, nose to nose he said, "Tomorrow at dawn we meet. I will have my day defending my sister's honor, and you, sir, will meet a fitting end for a reprobate."

Gabe turned to Eloise, his heart aching with the pain he'd caused her. She looked lost and confused, and he had hurt her. "Let me explain, it is not as bad as Fenshaw makes out."

"Pistols at dawn," Fenshaw said, giving no quarter on his stance.

"It's illegal to duel," Eloise said, looking at Fenshaw. "You kill a duke and you'll end up hanging on the ropes like the men who rot in Newgate."

Fenshaw shrugged, a mad gleam to his eyes. "If death is what it takes for my sister's honor to be restored, then I will gladly face the consequences. The Duke of Dale wronged our family and will pay dearly for his sins."

At the man's ignorance Gabe's temper snapped. "I never knew she was your sister, and when I did, it was too late to repair the damage I had done."

"That does not make your actions right," Eloise said to him, her brow furrowed. "A servant is someone in your care, a worker who should be protected from harm and treated with respect." A tear slipped free. "I do not know who you are."

Gabe swallowed and pulled forth all the ducal breeding he had in him. "I am Dale. Your betrothed, should I need to remind you."

"I cannot marry you."

Her lip quivered and Gabe fought the urge to wrap her in his arms. Knew any attempt to comfort her would be met with disdain and loathing. "And why is that?"

"You lie," she said. "Lie about everything. About who you are and what you have done. I don't know you at all. And I will not marry you. I'm sorry."

Gabe watched the woman he loved walk down the darkened passage and wondered how the hell he was going to get her back. He turned and looked at Fenshaw, then allowed all the rage he had controlled for the past few minutes to come to the fore. "Pistols at dawn it is. Putney Heath, if you will."

"I will indeed. My second will be in touch." Fenshaw bowed and followed Eloise into the ballroom.

Gabe ran a hand through his hair and cursed. What a mess he'd made of it all, and now, after not even a day in London, and he had lost the only woman he'd ever loved.

Damnation.

CHAPTER 8

"He's a liar and a despoiler of innocent women." Eloise wiped her nose with the back of her hand. Her life was over. To find Gabe again, only to lose him, was too much to bear. How she could ever forgive his indiscretions was unimaginable. "You do not know that." Emma sat beside her. "Listen, I spoke to Bertie at the ball, and from what I could persuade him to tell me, His Grace may not be totally to blame."

Eloise met her friend's consoling gaze and sniffed. "He slept with Lord Fenshaw's sister and left her with child. How can he not be blamed for such roguish behaviour?"

Emma handed her a handkerchief. "Miss Fenshaw's mind was disordered, from what I can gather. She ran away from her brother's estate, and, for some perplexing reason, sought work in the guise of a maid. The duke was a young man then, and although I do not condone his actions toward his staff, perhaps they had formed a tendre of some kind. He is not a vicious or unkind person. Their relationship was a mistake, a youthful folly. Promise, before you act hastily, you will speak to him. Find out what further truths need be told. You love him, and you have a chance at happiness. Do not throw it away."

Eloise stared silently at the unlit marble hearth. "You mentioned she was institutionalized. Do you truly believe she was inflicted with some sort of madness?"

Emma stood and pulled the bell cord for the servants. "I do believe so. I recall Miss Fenshaw during our season, was forever tipping her nose at the ton and its strictures. Forever in some sort of trouble, exhibiting bizarre behaviours. She had a terrible time of it."

The butler entered. "My lady?"

"Tea, Peter, and could you have Cook make up a cold compress please?"

"What's the compress for?" Eloise asked.

"Your eyes." Emma smiled. "We cannot have you speaking to the Duke of Dale looking like a bloated fish that has been for sale too long at the fishmonger."

Eloise touched the swollen skin about her face and knew it would look blotchy and red. Nerves fluttered in her stomach over her impending discussion with the duke. So much rested on his answers, most importantly, their future happiness. Was this past transgression a terrible error, he, as a young man, could not set right? And if he felt no guilt, why flee the country for years? Unfortunately, his actions indicated both shame and guilt. None of it made any sense, and she wished she had stayed to hear him out.

Foolish, hasty, headstrong woman.

"He is to duel tomorrow. I must go. I need to speak to His Grace and convince him to do otherwise. Perhaps now Lord Fenshaw has had some hours to mull things over, he may no longer wish to face his nemesis at dawn."

Emma frowned, directed a maid to place the tea dishes before her, and held out the cold compress. "Not before you hold this to your face for a time. Your eyes are dreadfully red, my dear. Only when I deem you appropriate for company, may you leave."

Eloise lay back with the cooling cloth on her face as directed. "Did anyone ever tell you what a saviour you are? You'll make a good mama, Emma."

"Thank you, dearest." Eloise heard the smile in her voice. "Now, enough sentimental talk, you'll make me cry."

"Very well. I'll not say another word." Eloise buttoned her lips and chuckled.

Gabe left for Putney Heath within an hour of leaving the Durham's ball. He wanted to get a feel for the location that might be the place of his demise. The carriage rumbled over the cobbled streets of Mayfair before passing through the more unsavoury locales of London, the stink and rot of its inhabitants prevalent on every street corner.

He frowned at the despicable living conditions and wondered how he could help to improve their lives, should he survive the morning's meeting.

"So it's all over between you and Lady Eloise then?"

Gabe turned away from the dimly lit streets and faced Hamish, his second and midshipman. "I'll tell you tomorrow after I face Fenshaw."

Hamish waved his concerns away. "You're a crack shot. No harm will befall ye."

He could only hope his friend's insight would prove true. Adventure on the high seas, which, many a time, involved armed pillage of English ships, once held his soul enrapt. Made him feel alive, and allowed him to take revenge on a country that had wronged him. But those were the brash exploits of his youth; Gabe found he no longer held such sentiments. Amazed he wasn't dead already from such actions.

Eloise was everything to him, and he would rather die than live without her. "Fenshaw is a good shot, from what I can recall, and he'll be aiming to injure me." Gabe sighed and rubbed his eyes. No, Fenshaw would not wish to injure him, kill him would be closer to the truth.

"Can ye speak to him and talk sense into him?"

He shook his head. "There's no talking sense to him." Gabe's laugh sounded far from humorous. "I tried speaking to him years ago before I left England, and the bastard wouldn't listen. No, I'll have to face him and hope for the best."

Hamish frowned. "What of the duchy should you die? What of ye ship?"

A twinge of guilt settled in Gabe's gut at the thought. He had despised the title and all it involved. Dale, such a proud and honourable name. Second son that he was, he had only brought scandal to the ducal door, tarnishing the family name. Or so his father always believed. Gabe had tried to right the wrong he had caused, but nothing could calm the wrath of his father. Nor could he find Fenshaw's sister to offer for her. Instead, he'd been ordered out of England by an irate father with a demand never to return.

"I should have stayed and fixed this error of judgement years ago. I was a foolish young man who should have known better. Had I tried harder, I could have found Miss Fenshaw. Explained better to father what had happened and what I intended to do to solve the problem." Gabe looked at the box of duelling pistols at his side, his finger absently stroking the wooden casing. "And now it is too late."

"Whatever the future holds, I wish you to know, working under you and being your friend was a privilege.

Rest assured, all will be well. You'll more than likely find when we make the Green Man Inn in an hour or so, Fenshaw is nowhere to be found."

Gabe nodded and returned to looking out the window; the bleakness of the streets matched his mood exactly, but he doubted his friends words. Fenshaw would be there intent on seeking his misbegotten revenge. That there was no doubt.

"He's gone. Already?"

"Yes, Lady Eloise. If you would please enter, I'm sure we can discuss your concerns further, inside." The old butler looked up the street, his eyes darting about, no doubt terrified someone would see her at the dukes door causing strife.

Eloise gave the elderly butler a frantic shake of her head. "No, no. I must go now. I have to reach him before it's too late."

She turned and ran down the front steps.

"To Putney," she called to her driver as she climbed back in her coach. "And please hurry."

She sank back against the plush seat, twisting her hands in her lap. She would be too late, she was sure of it. Already, the night sky had started to give way to the dawn. Had she lost the opportunity to speak to Gabe again, she would never forgive Emma for it. Why didn't her friend wake her when she'd fallen asleep on the settee? Eloise moved to the opposite seat and opened the little window between herself and her driver. "Is this the fastest you can go?"

"Aye, my lady. Any faster and I'm likely to turn us over at the next corner."

With a snap, she shut the portal. Taking a deep breath,

Eloise attempted to calm herself. At this early hour, not many people were on the London streets; they would make it in time. They had to.

The nightmare that had awoken her haunted her mind. Gabe, bleeding and lying dead on the heath…alone. She shut her eyes, not able to bear such a thought. He had wronged, but he was barely a man when he had done so. The fault lie with them both, Gabe and Miss Fenshaw, and he would explain. Eloise was sure.

Should he live to do so…

The carriage rolled around a corner, and she clasped the strap to keep her upright, the steel object in her pocket digging into her thigh.

Fenshaw was mad. Perhaps the affliction that affected his sister ran in his family's blood. Whatever the reason, she did not trust the man to honour the rules of duelling. Her dream had been so vivid and lifelike. No, she would not allow Fenshaw to kill the man she loved.

If anyone was to mete out punishment to Gabe, she deserved the right. He had lied to her. Lied repeatedly, and yet, only to save her from truths that would hurt—had hurt her. She herself was not entirely honest when she'd first met him. Had she not looked at him with longing no virginal maiden should ever know, asked him to teach her to shoot a gun when she could hit a small mark accurately at a hundred yards?

Trivial lies, but lies just the same.

By the time they pulled across from Putney Heath, the birds were singing a tune to the new day. The glow of dawn painted the horizon, dimming her hope of arriving in time.

"Come, we must hurry." Her driver jumped down from the box and ran behind her toward a park. Eloise looked about, not really knowing where she was going. They would have to be around here somewhere.

"'Tis nearly dawn, my lady."

"I know." She inwardly cursed the reminder. Bad enough they were duelling at all. Men and their stupid rules of honor. Whatever was wrong with discussing one's problems like the gentlemen they were supposed to be? Two shots sounded behind a copse of trees just ahead of them. Eloise slid to a stop. Her blood ran cold in her veins, and, picking up her skirts, she ran.

At the sight that beheld her, Eloise, without hesitation, pulled out her flintlock, aimed, and fired at Fenshaw. The man had wounded the duke, and against all rules, was taking aim to shoot him again. Relief poured over her like a balm when her shot sent his lordship's gun flying from his hand, split in two pieces.

Gabe instinctively ducked at the sound of a second gunshot. He turned to see Fenshaw clasping his hand, another pistol shattered at his feet. Confused, he scanned the park, then stilled at the sight of Eloise. Gun still pointed, smoke billowing about her like an avenging angel. At that moment, he knew she was

Indeed a seraph. One who had saved his life. Guilt over Fenshaw's sister or a warped sense of honour had made Gabe fire over Fenshaw's head. He'd planned to accept whatever punishment providence dealt him, but apparently, Fenshaw had not been satisfied with his initial effort and thought to twist fate to meet his own agenda.

Fenshaw's second kicked his friend's gun away and helped the man toward his carriage.

Gabe called after him. "My apologies, Fenshaw. What happened between your sister and me…I made a mistake, and I wish I could repair the damage I did, but I cannot."

Eloise came and stood beside him, her eyes wide with concern at the wound to his arm. "I would have married her," he said and heard a growl of displeasure from Eloise.

Fenshaw halted his retreat. "Bollocks," he said in a menacing tone. "You used her, then left her defenceless. Carrying your child."

"You are wrong. When your sister confessed her condition, I told her I would support her, make her and the child comfortable for the rest of her days. She fled that night. For weeks, I searched but could find no trace of her. Only when my man notified me of her whereabouts and her true identity did I realize what I must do. I came to see you, but you would not admit me. I wrote to you requesting her hand in marriage, but by then, you had shipped her off to an asylum."

"Where you left her to die," Fenshaw said through clenched teeth.

Gabe looked at the man with disgust. Pigheaded bastard. "No, Fenshaw, you left her to die. I tried to right my wrongs. You wouldn't hear of it. Instead, you spread lies about town of my misdemeanour and sullied my name."

"And you left England because of it all." Eloise clasped his arm and frowned. "Oh, Gabe, I'm so sorry I didn't give you a chance to explain."

"I was ordered to leave. My father made it patently obvious he wished never to see me again. He was granted his wish when he died two years ago."

"I'm so sorry." Eloise hugged him, needing to hear his wonderful heart beat beneath his shirt.

He shrugged as he watched Fenshaw climb into his carriage. "You have no reason to apologize."

The doctor, summoned by Gabe's second, waddled over to him, opening his bag as he came. "Shall I have a look at the wound, Your Grace?"

With the help of Eloise, Gabe struggled out of his ruined jacket. The red stain covered most of his left arm, but the injury itself when revealed was only a flesh wound.

The doctor ripped the shirtsleeve away and bandaged his arm. "This should suffice until your return to London. Send for your usual doctor to see to it. Should have a thorough cleaning before it's bandaged again."

"Of course, thank you, doctor." Eloise shook the man's hand.

Noting her paleness, Gabe grimaced, his heart thumping hard against his ribs. He loved her, could see this morning's events had rattled her usual steadfast resolve.

"Very good," the doctor said and bowed. "Good day to you, Your Grace, my lady."

They were silent for a moment before Gabe led Eloise toward his carriage, before he realized he had one more item of business to attend. He turned to his second. "My time on the seas has come to an end, my friend. And so the ship is yours to do with as you please."

Hamish, who was packing up the pistols stilled at his words. "You're giving me the ship?"

Gabe smiled at his friends shock. The man was more than worthy of such a gift, having a steadfast character and generous soul. He didn't know a lot about the fellow, where he came from or how he came to be working for him, but having spent the past two years at sea he knew a great man when he met one, and Hamish Doherty was exactly that. "I am." He looked down at Eloise. "My life is in London now, and it is where I belong. But should you ever need me, you know where I am."

"I don't know what to say," Hamish said.

"No need to say anything, my friend. I wish you well." Gabe helped Eloise up into the carriage. He took a calming breath, the smell of the cool morning air brought his life back into focus. That he was alive was a bonus he had not thought possible only hours before. Now, however, beside the woman he loved, everything fell into place. For the first time in his life, Gabe felt free of scandal. Ready to do justice to his title and to the huge estates he had inherited. "Ride with me back to London?"

She nodded, her dark hair, tied by a loose piece of ribbon, shining in the early sunlight. Gabe shut the door behind them, forgetting his wound, and winced.

Eloise shifted to his side. "Does it pain you?" Her brow furrowed; her bottom lip captured by her teeth. An overwhelming urge to capture her delicious lips overrode all his thoughts of decency.

Gabe tilted her chin and looked into eyes as green as the rainforests of South America. "Kiss me."

"But your arm," she said, sliding a fraction closer.

"Is fine." Gabe bent and took her lips, allowed all he felt for her to come out in the kiss. Hesitant at first, Eloise soon forgot his injury, forgot where they were, who they were and matched his desire. Her tongue stroked his and sent fire shooting through his body.

Lifting her onto his lap, Gabe set about teasing her, giving her pleasure before the tree-lined streets of Mayfair ended their interlude. Not a moment wasted as he supped from her lips, curled his hand about her back, and held her tight against him. Her breasts rubbed his chest, the pebbled peaks straining against her morning gown.

He clasped the strap and held them both upright as the carriage lurched around a corner. Her chuckle brought a smile to his lips.

"We cannot make love here." She chuckled when his hand curved about her breast and kneaded.

"What about sex. Would you be willing to do that here?" Gabe bent his head and took a nipple into his mouth. Allowed his tongue to swirl, his teeth to nibble and tease her into agreement.

Her hands clasped his hair, and Gabe knew she was fighting her own sense of decency.

"My, that feels good."

Gabe set to work on her other breast. "Have you missed me then?"

"You know I have." Eloise squirmed off his lap, turned, and straddled his legs.

Gabe lifted her skirts as she settled about his shaft now straining against his breeches, all but begging for release.

When she reached down and rubbed his engorged cock, Gabe swallowed and tried to pull what was left of his self-control together. Her delicate fingers played to a tune his body knew and remembered well. "I want you, now and always," he said on a gasp when her deft fingers opened his front falls and stroked flesh against flesh.

"I know." The seductive glint in her eyes only confirmed her words. The sex they had enjoyed on the boat was always wild and hot. Gabe could hardly name one place where they hadn't fucked hard and fast but always to the enjoyment of them both.

It seemed nothing had changed. No matter where they were or what they did, pleasure and fulfilment was paramount. And love. Always love.

Eloise rubbed her wet, heated core against his rod, and Gabe hissed in a breath. "Do that again."

She did, and he moaned. He pulled her close and, taking her eager lips, pushed his pants out of the way and released his cock, lifted Eloise, and slid into her heated depths.

"Gabe…"

He nipped her throat, wiggled down the seat, and allowed her to ride him. She was a goddess before him. Hair cascaded over her shoulders, barely hiding the breasts he had freed. The plump globes swayed with their lovemaking, tempting him like a child in a sweet shop.

"I love making love with you." She ran her hands against his chest, her fingers finding his nipple beneath his shirt and grazing it with her nails.

With barely suppressed excitement, Gabe watched Eloise sit upright and lick two fingers, her eyes wicked with intent. His balls tightened, his cock expanded when she trailed her hand down her body to rest against her sex. A soft moan expelled from her parted lips when she touched herself, stroked the little nubbin he so loved to kiss. Lick. Savour.

The sight of her touching herself was more than he could stand. With a swiftness that surprised him, Gabe flipped her over onto the squabs, lifted her legs about his waist, and took her. Fucked her. Pressed hard against her sex, and watched as her eyes glazed over with wonder and pleasure that ricocheted through them both.

Their gasps and moans echoed throughout the carriage, heedless of the driver who could overhear. Her hot core pulled and contracted about him, draining him of every ounce of life.

"Marry me," he asked at length, leaning over her to watch the woman he loved come back from the exquisite state they always achieved together.

"Why?" Eloise asked, a grin on her succulent lips.

"Because I love you. Need you. Cannot possibly live without you." He leaned down and brushed his lips against hers. "Besides, you saved my life, and now I owe you mine."

Eloise made an agreeable noise at his words and wrapped her arms about his neck. "How could I refuse the captain of my hearts' order?"

"This is no captain's order, my love, but a duke's heartfelt wish."

"Oh, Gabe." She pulled him against her and held him close. "I will marry you, captain, duke, whatever you wish to be. I'll be yours, for now and for always."

He grinned and pushed his now very erect rod against her heat. "I'm having a feeling you need to be mine, again."

Eloise's chuckle rumbled against his chest as she kissed his sweat-streaked skin. "Now would be perfect," she purred, sliding her legs up against his hips, opening for him.

Perfect indeed.

EPILOGUE

Eloise walked toward Gabe in the great library of his ancestral home and smiled at the man she would soon call husband. His attire fitted him like a glove, left little to her imagination to what delights sat beneath the superfine coat and breeches.

Before the gathered guests, only the few they wished to share in their special day, they said their marriage vows. Promised each other to a lifetime of love.

It was a perfect morning for a wedding and she couldn't have asked for a better man who stood watching her, his gaze boring into her as if she were the most precious piece of artwork in the room.

Her trip to the wilds of another country with her brother, the heartbreak she'd endured there eased when she'd met Gabe. She was a fortunate woman who would be loved unconditionally for the rest of her life.

She smiled.

. . .

That night Eloise waited for Gabe in his ducal bedroom. The dark wooden bed bore silk curtains that billowed in the fragrant spring air. It made her feel mysterious and seductive. She could hear him talking to his valet as he dressed for bed and she smiled. He had no need for drawers this evening.

The door from the dressing room swung open and Gabe nonchalantly leaned against the threshold. His body was bare from the waist up, and with the flitting moonlight that filtered through the windows, every contour on his well, defined body was hers to admire.

Her body hummed with eagerness to have him close. Over the last few days they'd been separated for the first time since Gabe had landed back in England. And every hour had seemed like a year. "Hello husband."

He pushed away from the door and strolled toward her. The muscles on his abdomen flexed and her mouth dried. He was a sight she was sure she'd never cease looking at.

"Good evening, wife." He crawled over her onto the bed, his hands either side of her face. "Have I told you how beautiful you look today?"

She grinned at his attempt of flattery, which utterly worked wonders on her expectant body. "More times than I can count." She cradled his hips and felt along the taut muscles that ran along his spine. Gabe had a lovely back, strong and straight and gorgeous to watch when he was busy doing manual tasks.

He took her lips and she inwardly sighed. Each stoke of tongue, each sup of her lips left her needy and hot. Within moments the kiss turned scorching, no longer beckoning but demanding, urging her to meet his desire.

Eloise did. She kissed back with all the love, desire and

lust she felt for this man. A man who was so much more than she'd ever expected to have in a husband.

She was a very lucky woman.

Her fingers met the band of his drawers and she pushed them off his hips, using her leg to slide them down to his feet. He chuckled through the kiss before pulling back.

"Is there something you're after, Your Grace?"

She started at the use of her new title then laughed. "Only you. Only ever you."

"I'm glad to hear it." With one swoop, he rolled onto his back and pulled her atop to straddle him. Eloise caught his eye and slowly, slipped her shift off over her head. His heated gaze could scorch skin, she was sure. "Like what you see?"

His hands slid up her waist and flexed over her breasts. His fingers paying homage to her nipples that beaded like hard little sweets just for him. "Very much so."

Gabe went to place her over his jutting cock, but Eloise shook her head. "Not so fast, Duke. I have other ideas for us tonight."

He raised his brows and grinned. "Then please proceed." He placed his hands under his head and watched her.

Eloise felt under the pillow and caught the silk tie she'd hidden there earlier. Pulling it out, she waved it before his face. "Give me your hands."

Gabe made a guttural sound of approval before doing as she asked. She tied them together quickly before lifting them above his head and tying him to the headboard. Her breasts rubbed against his face and she sucked in a startled breath when she felt his tongue lather at one nipple.

Sitting back, she took the opportunity to run her hands

over his chest, his stomach, his jutting cock that sat in wait, hard and heavy in her hands.

"What are you going to do to me?" His arms flexed against her ties and she smiled.

"You should be asking what I'm not going to do." Eloise slid down his body, watched as his eyes widened as her mouth came to sit directly over his cock.

She licked the droplet of come at the end of his penis before suckling the head into her mouth. He groaned, lifting his body a little to push further into her mouth. Wanting to please him as he always pleased her, she clasped his cock in her hand and stroked. With each glide of her fingers he hardened even more, making his thick shaft stand to attention.

Eloise took him fully into her mouth, swirled her tongue about his length as her hand worked him to a frenzy. He groaned, sucked in startled breaths as with each pull and glide of her mouth, she pushed him ever closer to release.

To have such a virile, strong man, squirming in desire, the need she could sense he had for her was the most erotic elixir she'd ever tasted. And tonight was just the start of many more days and night with this man.

Her heart sang with the joy of it.

Sucking harder, she increased her speed and soon had him near the release he craved. Sitting up, she continued to stroke him slower while watching his ragged breathing calm a little.

"What are you doing?"

"Teasing you." She ran her tongue over his penis once more before kissing and nibbling her way up his abdomen. Each taut muscle she kissed, nipped and kissed better before coming to the sensitive spot beneath his ear he loved her kissing most.

"I want to make you burn for me."

She heard the ties flex against the headboard. "I want to fuck you."

His smutty words only made her want him to fuck her as well. But not yet. "Then my plan is working." She placed her mons over his penis and rubbed him against her sex. She was wet and ready, her sex aching with a need to be fulfilled by him. And soon, she promised herself, she would have her wish.

Eloise sat up and without letting him enter her, rubbed his engorged member against her, over and over again she slid against his heat, teased them both to distraction before they were both panting hard, their bodies close to climax but not willing to let go of the delicious ecstasy they always found in each other's arms.

"Fuck me, Eloise."

She smiled and impaled herself on his cock. They moaned in unison as she leaned on his chest and rode him. Pushed them both onward, toward to the divine end they craved. Gabe moaned her name, his arms fighting against his imprisonment. Eloise enjoyed every moment of having him at her mercy. She slowed their lovemaking when necessary and sped it up when she liked. Her body was so close, but her mind wanted to continue the erotic torture.

All through her core she felt her orgasm flow through her. Her body shook as Gabe thrust hard into her sex and pushed her orgasm to peak just as he too found his release. Her eyes fluttered open just as she realized Gabe had freed himself from his bonds.

He rolled her over and pinned her beneath him. "Did you enjoy yourself?"

Her body felt groggy with satisfaction. She chuckled. "I really did. It's enjoyable having you at my mercy. I may have to do that again."

He licked his lips and she inwardly groaned. He was truly too delicious for words. "As long as I can do it to you too."

Hmm. Never had a question been so tempting. "Starting from now?"

"Hell yes. Right now, my little minx. Now put your hands above your head and enjoy."

She did as she was told and settled in for another wondrous orgasm. "I love you," she said, feeling tears well at the fortunate place she now found herself.

"And I you," he replied, before making good on his promise to please her. And please her he did.

Always.

A MARRIAGE MADE IN MAYFAIR

Scandalous London, Book 3

※

Miss Suzanna March wished for one thing: the elusive, rakish charmer, Lord Danning. But after a frightful first season such dreams are impossible. That is until she returns to London, a new woman, and one who will not let the ton's dislike of her stand in her way of gaining what she wants: revenge on the Lord who gave her the cut direct...

Lord Danning, unbeknown to his peers, is in financial strife and desperate to marry an heiress. Such luck would have it Miss Suzanna March fits all his credentials and seduction in his plan of action. Yes, the woman who returned from Paris is stronger, defiant, and a little argumentative, but it does not stop Lord Danning finding himself in awe and protective of her.

But will Suzanna fall for such pretty words from a charmer? Or will

Lord Danning prove to Suzanna and himself that she is more than his ticket out of debtor's prison...?

CHAPTER 1

"Are you sure you want to do this, Suzanna?" asked Henry, as he watched her preparations from the doorway.

"Of course. I'm sure. Lord Danning may have frightened me off last season, but he'll not do it again." She shifted her gaze away from her brother as her French maid Celeste pinned a curl to dangle alluringly over her ear.

Henry pushed himself away from the doorframe and strolled over to where she sat in front of her dressing table. He held out his hand and pulled Suzanna to her feet, twirling her slowly as he admired her. "Well, you'll certainly turn heads at the ball. Celeste has worked miracles. I hardly recognize my clumsy, unfashionable little sister."

Suzanna glanced at her reflection—nothing about this sophisticated woman staring back at her resembled the humiliated, heartbroken debutante who ran, not only from a ballroom, but also from the country.

Gone were the orange locks that had hung with no life about her shoulders and the eyebrows that were forever in need of plucking. Even the little mole above her lip looked delicate and not at all unattractive, as some matrons had once pointed out.

Oh yes, she would draw attention tonight, but if truth be told, there was only one head she really wanted to turn.

"You like this new look, Mademoiselle March?" asked Celeste.

Her eyes sparkled with expectation. "I do." She laughed. "Oh, Celeste, thank you so very much. You have outdone yourself."

And Royce Durnham, Viscount Danning, could grovel at her silk slippers for all she cared. A grin quirked her lips over the thought of seeing one of London's most powerful men clasping her skirts, tears welling in his eyes begging for forgiveness. It would only serve him right, especially after the atrocious set-down bestowed on her last year at her coming out.

Celeste clucked in admonishment. "My profession is so much easier when one has so beautiful a canvas with which to work. I only make improvement with what is before me."

"Too true," Henry stated, kissing his sister's cheek.

Suzanna laughed. Perhaps they were right. For it was *she* who stared back with green eyes so large they seemed to pale the freckles across her nose to insignificance. "I can only hope my deportment has also improved. I was such a calamity last season."

"Was your first season, *oui?*"

"Yes." Suzanna walked over to the window and looked out onto the grounds of her father's London townhouse. "Father having made his money in trade ensured my lack of popularity. I was certainly not fit for some of the mamas of the *ton*." She shrugged away the stinging memory of their rejection. The worst had come from the lofty Lord

Danning, a rich, powerful aristocrat, tall with an athletic frame that bespoke of hours in the saddle. He was a gentleman who always dressed in immaculate attire that fitted his body like a kid leather glove, but without the airs of a dandy.

Even the memory of a strong jaw and dark-blue eyes made her belly clench with longing. He was the embodiment of everything one looked for in a husband—until he opened his mouth, spoke, and ruined all such musings.

"Your father was knighted, mademoiselle. Surely, the English aristocracy would not slight your family's humble beginnings. Everyone must start somewhere. *No?*"

"You are right, Celeste, yet perhaps if it had been a more distant relation than my father who made our fortune, the *ton* may have been more favourable toward me. No matter my obscene dowry, they did not welcome me as warmly as some of the other girls."

Henry growled his disapproval. "I'll meet you downstairs, Suzanna, before my temper is unleashed on the *ton's* ideals. Aunt Agnes will be down soon to accompany us, so do not delay." He marched from the room.

"I'll be down shortly." Suzanna sat at her desk and picked up her quill, idly rolling it between her fingers. She was glad she had thought to write to Victoria. Her dearest and best friend would ensure she arrived tonight at the Danning's ball in the company of friends.

"I'll wear the light green silk tonight, Celeste," she said, placing the quill onto the desk. "And Mary," she said to her second maid who fluttered about, tidying the room. "Could you bring my supper up to my bedchamber straightaway? I don't have much time to get ready."

Her maid curtsied and departed. Celeste pulled her gown from the armoire. "There is a small wrinkle, mademoiselle. I will take it downstairs and quickly press it. Your hair and lips, I will repair when you have finished the supper. *Oui?*"

Suzanna smiled. "Thank you. I must admit to being a little excited about going. It has been months since I was in London, and the ball is supposed to be the event of the season."

"And you, mademoiselle, will be the most beautiful of all!"

Suzanna chuckled as the door closed behind her servant. The most beautiful; well, perhaps this once. Maybe if she acted with all the decorum and manners hammered into her over the last few months, a man might magically fall at her feet with an offer of marriage. At one and twenty, marriage was certainly what one ought to think on. Just not with Lord Danning. Not any more, at least.

Hateful cad.

CHAPTER 2

"Lord Danning, allow me to explain once more. The cost of running your thoroughbred breeding programme, the living expenses on your estates here in England and Italy, along with your excessive lifestyle, are leaving you very short on funds.

"I'm sorry to be the one to tell you such unwelcome news, but the extreme way of life you and your brother—whom you fund—live, has finally taken a toll. You have three months at most to settle the debts of your family, or I'm afraid you are facing debtors' prison."

Royce swore and slumped back in his chair. He glanced up at the harsh, no-nonsense visage of his solicitor, Mr. Andrews, and cringed. He had expected this meeting would not be to his liking. But such news as his ruination was not quite what he'd imagined.

"Can I not sell off more of my estate?"

"What remains of the property is entailed for future generations. You have already sold off what you could. Furnishings, material objects will only buy you weeks at the most. Of course, any *family* pieces must remain with the estate." Mr. Andrews paused. "Perhaps you could sell off the hunters and some equipages, my lord? Or the property in Rome?"

Royce halted the drumming of his fingers against the table. "You mock me, sir? Broke I may be, but I'm still a lord with friends in high places. These same friends who would be willing to cease using your services should I tell them you have lost your senses. Sell off my carriages and horseflesh. Whoever heard of such a preposterous idea?"

"Apologies, my lord, but again, I must speak frankly. As your financial counsellor, I must advise closing down the London home, or better yet, renting it out for the season and returning to your country estate."

"What?" Royce asked, his voice harder than it ought to be against the man. Mr. Andrews was only doing his job after all. He gritted his teeth, calming his ire.

"For months, my lord, I cautioned you, warned you this would occur, and yet you ignored me. You must rein in the excessive expenditures your family can no longer afford. Your name is an asset in the *ton*; use it, and procure a rich wife. My apologies for speaking out of turn."

"You think you're the only one who is displeased? I'm a Danning, proud of my lineage, and the blood of the great men that flows through my veins. A family line handed down unblemished from father to son. And now, I, the current viscount, protector of my family, could lose it all."

Royce stood and strode over to the decanter of brandy. His hands shook as he poured the fiery liquid. The burning sting of the drink warmed his belly, yet his body remained cold.

"What do I do?" The life he lived could not be over. To lose one's station in life was beyond imagining. He could not be...poor! The thought of debtor's prison, where lice and fleas were as common as a cellmate, sent a shiver of revulsion down his spine.

"As I said, marry an heiress. And be quick about it, mind."

Royce placed his second glass of brandy upon the sideboard and frowned. "I had not thought of such a possibility." His solicitor threw him a sceptical look. "Well, of course I've thought of marriage, just not marriage to a wealthy woman. We Dannings have always been comfortable with our financial position; marrying for money has never been a priority for me." Royce paused in thought. "Certainly it would allow the family to continue to live on as before." His solicitor made a choking sound, his plump chin meeting his chest in disapproval. "You wish to say something further, Mr. Andrews."

"Your family cannot continue spending, my lord. The income you procure from your estate is not enough to cover your expenditures with your horses, let alone season after season of spending as if money is no object. Your investment income from the East India Company has yet to arrive and may not for many months. You make no money, my lord. Certainly not enough to keep you in the current lifestyle you lead. Your brother especially cannot continue with his life as it is now. He exceeds his monthly income tenfold, which you pay whenever a debtor knocks on your door."

Mr. Andrews cleared his throat and met his gaze squarely. "If you wish to secure the well-being of your future children, limitations must be put in place and adhered to."

Royce bowed his head. The old solicitor was right. His brother would have to be brought to heel, and along with it his own expenditures.

"Right, then. I'm sure I can bring order to the family's

troubles...and my brother," he said, forming a plan in his mind. "Well, I'd best be preparing for the ball."

"A ball, my lord? Excuse me for speaking out again, but you cannot possibly afford to throw a ball. If I may make another suggestion—best you procure an Almack's voucher, and make an appearance at the patroness's expense," Mr. Andrews said, bending down to place his papers into his leather carry bag.

"Mr. Andrews, you are well aware I throw the ball of the season every year. One no one would miss. Why, have you not noticed my staff bustling about, busy with the preparations?" Royce strode toward the door. "I'm sure, though as my new financial situation is not yet known, there will be many a young filly entering my door, eager to marry a viscount. I shall simply favour only those of sufficient wealth."

"Sounds like a marriage made in heaven, my lord."

"No." Royce grinned. "A marriage made in Mayfair."

With a curt nod, his solicitor slapped on his hat, tapped the top, and left.

Royce leaped up the stairs and sauntered toward his living quarters. The old codger had finally proved worthy. The idea of courting an heiress was just what he needed. Perhaps his brother would follow suit and marry one as well. Then at least George wouldn't be pulling on his coat tails every week for more coin.

The thought of never being plump in the pocket again sent a shiver of revulsion down his spine. All the Dannings before him, generations of wealthy English lords, would rise up from their graves in protest should he fail to marry well and lose his estate.

Well, he wouldn't allow such a thing.

He would find a woman, marry her, and ensure that his family's future was secure.

Royce pulled at his cravat and rang for his valet, his thoughts absorbed with the guests due to arrive at his home for the ball tonight.

Those of the highest peerage with money enough to please the monarchy would attend. Surely a wife could be found amongst the pretty women who will undoubtedly fall at his feet.

Begging to be his countess and wife.

CHAPTER 3

Suzanna nodded her thanks as she passed a flute of champagne to her friend. The ball was a crush, full to the brim with the *ton's* highest patrons, many of whom looked down their noses at the young heiress.

"It's extremely warm in here tonight," Victoria said, fanning herself with a silk fan that matched her dress. "I believe I may have to walk the terrace soon, or I'm certain I may faint."

"Do you intend to walk out there alone?" Suzanna laughed at the crimson blush that stole over her friend's cheeks.

"No, I'll have you by my side." She gestured toward the card room door not far from where they stood. "I see Viscount Danning is extremely dashing this eve. Never have I seen such a fine piece of masculinity within the *ton*, and so attentive to the ladies, if I may say so."

Suzanna gazed over at the man she had followed like a ninny hammer last season. She threw him a baleful glare she hoped pricked his senses and hurt every fiber of his being. Not that he was looking her way, of course. Seemed nothing had changed in the year she'd been away. Being from trade, as she was deemed, wasn't of course worth admiring. "Yes." Suzanna took a sip of her drink. "He seems as stiff and as cold as ever."

Victoria chuckled. "Oh, I don't know. I think he seems...kind of sad tonight as if he's lost his best friend, or some such."

"I didn't know Lord Danning was capable of having a best friend."

"Oh, Suzanna, you are too cruel."

Something in her friend's tone made her senses bristle. "I didn't know you cared a fig what Lord Danning felt." She turned and looked at her.

Victoria blushed an even darker shade of crimson and waved her remark aside. "No, of course I do not. He is nothing to me. I was merely making a general observation."

Suzanna turned her gaze back to his lordship and wondered what had caused this sullen frown on his normally attractive features.

"And anyway, to term Lord Danning as cold and stiff is a little cruel. From memory I believe you named him the epitome of gentlemanly behaviour last season."

Suzanna inwardly cringed at the reminder. "I may have had such a ridiculous notion last year, but my thoughts are much altered this season, as you well know. I certainly do not think him so now."

Victoria touched her arm in a comforting gesture before her eyes widened and sparkled with joviality as she spied someone over Suzanna's shoulder. "Oh, here comes your brother. Do I appear well enough?"

"You are as beautiful as always," Suzanna said, as she turned toward her elder sibling.

With a sweeping bow, Henry took Victoria's hand then

kissed his sister's cheek. "May I say how beautiful you both look this eve, Suz, Lady Victoria." Her brother's gaze settled on Victoria with a twinkle in his dark green orbs.

She tittered, and Suzanna wondered when her brother would get up the courage to ask her dearest friend to marry him. Assuming she would be allowed to marry into gentry, one generation away from trade. Victoria, after all, was an earl's daughter.

"What brings you to our side, Henry? Come to sweep your wallflower sister from her seat and dance with her?"

"Of course I will dance with you, after I escort the delightful Lady Victoria out for the next set."

"I would like that very much, Mr. March," Victoria smiled, dazzling her brother once again.

Henry threw an exultant smile over his shoulder as they walked away. Alone, Suzanna sipped her drink and watched the dancers twirl and laugh on the ballroom floor. Many of the gentlemen here tonight had looked her way, but were yet to venture to her side. She checked her gown and touched her hair, making sure she didn't have anything out of place. Her Aunt Agnes smiled and waved from her situation, not a few seats away.

Suzanna smiled back and hoped she didn't disappoint her aunt with another disastrous season. Henry and she owed everything to their father's only living sister. After the tragic death of their parents in a carriage accident, Aunt Agnes had come to live with them and raised them as best she could.

Suzanna supposed her awkwardness in the *ton* could be due to the fact their aunt had grown up the daughter of a farmer and had never ventured into society. Not until Suzanna's father had made the sound investment in mining did the family start to move in different circles than those to which they were accustomed.

She looked at her Aunt Agnes and a lump formed in her throat. Her aunt also sat alone, preferring to speak little lest she say something that would cause strife for her charge. Love for the woman surged through Suzanna, and she promised herself this season would be different.

The humiliating memory of the Coots ball, when she'd walked from the retiring room with her gown askew, and showing enough ankle to make her red hair pale in comparison to her complexion, made her inwardly cringe.

What a horror last year's season was, certainly one to forget, and never to repeat. Surely after many months of learning to be a lady of the highest calibre she could manage to dance with someone other than her brother, and make her aunt happy.

"Good evening, Miss March."

Anyone, but him.

Suzanna swallowed a sip of champagne and watched Lord Danning bow, his dark, amused gaze looking up at her before he straightened. Her own narrowed.

"Evening, Lord Danning." *And I'm not at all in favour of speaking to you, you obnoxious rake, so please go away!*

"I hope you are well this eve, Miss March, and enjoying the ball?"

Suzanna barely stopped herself from rolling her eyes in disinterest at his contrived conversation. "I was enjoying it very well, my lord." *Until a minute or so ago.*

Lord Danning's lips twitched as if he understood her meaning. "I heard you travelled abroad over the past year?"

Suzanna pulled at the hem of her glove and met his lordship's gaze. "Yes, to Paris."

"You are much changed since I saw you last." His lordship handed her a glass of champagne and took her empty one without hesitation.

"I suppose you mean I'm no longer dressed like a disaster and my hair actually meets current fashion requirements."

He coughed. "I beg your pardon. Have I said something wrong, Miss March?"

Suzanna glanced at his immaculate attire with loathing. Damn the man to look perfect in every way. With very little effort, he always seemed able to appear pristine and relaxed. Yet Suzanna had to hire a French maid and take endless classes on deportment just so she could appear half respectable in society. She gritted her teeth at the vexing thought.

"I'm sorry, my lord, but I cannot understand why you are here talking to me. All you wished to say was more than adequately said last season, if I recall."

The colour drained from Lord Danning's face, leaving him a pasty shade of white. "Forgive me, Miss March. I was merely being polite. This is my ball, if you recall, and I do try to keep up with my duties as the host."

Suzanna smiled with no warmth behind the gesture. "Oh, I'm sure you were, my lord, but where your manners are concerned I care not."

His mouth gaped, reminding her of a fish. "You're angry with me." Lord Danning paused, his gaze speculative. "Why?"

"Why!" Suzanna shook her head at his question. Obviously, she was so unremarkable that their conversation in this very ballroom last year had been forgotten. "Perhaps you should seek out those who desire your company. I am not one of them."

He steered her behind a potted palm and hid her from the watchful eyes of the *ton*. Suzanna strove to calm her beating heart as the man she had longed for, wanted to kiss just once only months before, stared down at her with an emotion she could not place.

"You have changed not only your looks, Miss March. You seem to have procured a hatred for me while in Paris along with an uncommonly rude mouth."

Suzanna shut her gaping, *rude* mouth with a snap. "Rude, my lord? It is not I who is being rude. A gentleman who indicates he finds a woman's inner strength of character repulsive is the one being rude. Why don't you just admit you do not care for a woman who does not swoon at your feet, pining for a proposal of marriage?"

"I may have stated your mouth was uncommonly rude, but I did not say I found it repulsive, Miss March. If you would care to accompany me out to the terrace, I could show you just how non-repulsive I find your person."

Suzanna's feet, with a will of their own, stepped toward the terrace doors. Had she not wanted to have such a tryst with him last season? To kiss Lord Danning would be a dream come true. Heat stole up her neck at the resounding chuckle behind her before footfalls followed close on her heels.

The cool night air was a welcome balm when she stepped free of the ballroom crush. Strong fingers clasped her upper arm and pulled her toward a darkened stretch of the terrace.

An inner voice screamed at her to break free from his grasp and flee. Run as fast as she could from this bounder. But she would not. She would show the high and mighty Lord Danning what he had turned down and walked away from without a second thought. Tonight, it would be her opportunity to do the walking away. Excitement thrummed through her like a drug at the thought of her revenge, shallow as it was.

"You are very beautiful tonight," he said, coaxing her to sit on a stone seat hidden within an ivy-clad alcove.

"I do not need your praise, my lord. If you're going to kiss me, it would be wise to do so now before I return to the ballroom." Suzanna stiffened her spine and met his smiling gaze. He wouldn't be laughing for long.

"Last season, when I first saw you, ribbons and frills flying about you, I could not take my eyes from you."

Suzanna smiled and ran her hands up the lapels of his coat and noted the darkening of his eyes. "Because of the fright I made?"

"No." His attention fastened on her lips before slipping lower and admiring her person. "Because I saw the woman beneath all that decoration and knew I wanted her."

Suzanna ground her teeth, and raised his chin with one finger to bring his eyes back level to hers. "Why is it I find such words false, Lord Danning? Your actions and words last season spoke otherwise," she said in an accusing tone.

He shushed her and shifted her finger from his chin to his lips. Heat stole into her belly as his sinful lips kissed the tip of her finger, and her argument was lost to flame. Never had she experienced such a thing with a man, and as dreadfully wicked such a thought was, Suzanna couldn't help but wish for more of the same.

"They are the truth, whether you choose to believe them or not."

"Perhaps, my lord," she said, as she reclaimed her hand from his. "It is because you termed me from trade last season and not someone you wished to associate with, even as a friend."

How the memory of his hateful words hurt still. She beat back the urge to run, to get as far from this rogue as she could. To go to a place he could never hurt her with his lofty airs and opinions.

Never would she allow anyone to belittle her as he had, no matter their rank. Anger over the memory spiked her lust, and revenge simmered to a boil within her.

Lord Danning would pay.

Without hesitation, his lordship skimmed his lips against her throat, eliciting a sigh from Suzanna. Butterflies took flight in her belly, and her toes curled in her silk slippers.

"I do not recall mentioning your father's business dealings, Miss March. Are you certain I spoke so reprehensibly to you?"

"Yes," she said on a sigh, before clearing her throat. "Yes," she repeated, more strongly. "You did. And if they were not your exact words, it was what you implied."

"What am I implying now?"

Suzanna swallowed a moan and took her bottom lip between her teeth when his tongue slid up her neck, and he gently nibbled on her earlobe. *Oh dear, she should stop him now before they went any further, perhaps this kiss was a bad idea after all.* Her fingers curled about his lapels, pulling him closer. Lavender soap permeated the air along with a smell that was wholly Lord Danning, intoxicating and all male.

"You have the most exquisite skin, Miss March," he said, shifting closer and turning her toward him.

Suzanna's mouth dried when his hand clasped her hip, the silk of her gown no impediment to his ardent touch. His grasp slid downward to span her thigh where he lifted her leg slightly to sit higher against his own. It left her feeling open and vulnerable, and wholly excited.

Damn him.

"I want to kiss every inch of your skin."

A flush of heat rose under her gown with the thought. "I hope you are not planning to do such a thing here, my lord."

"No." He chuckled. "But perhaps we may find another secluded alcove where you will grant me such favours."

Suzanna shook her head. "I do not think so, my lord."

"Just a kiss then?" He pulled back and stared at her a moment. His gaze glistened with challenge in the dim light.

Suzanna chuckled. The laughing, teasing man before her reminded her of the Lord Danning she thought she knew and proclaimed a friend last season before his atrocious behaviour. Feelings she squashed rose within her, and so too, a pang of sadness; that although she would welcome his kiss, wished it in fact, she was not as fond of Lord Danning as one ought to be at such a moment. She could not quell her need to teach the high stickler a lesson he'd never forget in manners and in how to treat a lady.

"Just a kiss," she said.

It was far from just a kiss…

When his lips touched hers, Suzanna lost all memory of his slight, the harsh words spoken between them and her revenge. Gone was the lady who spent hours on deportment, hair, fashion, speech and anything else you could think of to be a diamond of the *ton*. In her place sat a woman who wanted the touch of a man. And not just any man, but Lord Danning.

The one man she no longer even liked.

CHAPTER 4

Royce clasped Suzanna's jaw and let his fingers slide into her hair. She was so altered since last year—lusciously thick strands of golden-red curls, now expertly coiffured to accentuate the greenest, brightest eyes he'd ever seen. He had noticed her immediately at her coming out ball. Fresh from the country, the woman had been awkward and unsure of herself, with no idea of her beauty. But her beauty was no longer hidden. Innocent longing, unlike any he'd ever known stared up at him and left him breathless.

His lips touched hers, and he was lost.

Royce allowed himself to be swept away into the firestorm of desire burning through his body. Never had soft lips and a tentative tongue excited him as much as it did now. He pulled her hard against him, and immediately, the intoxicating scent of jasmine enthralled him. Her ardent response to his kiss urged him to take the intimate interlude to a more satisfying conclusion, but the gentleman within him urged caution.

After his mistreatment of her last season, Suzanna

deserved more than a rough tumble in the vine. For all her untutored yet delicious kiss, she was untouched. Royce didn't yet know if she was a candidate for his future wife, but what he did understand was to gain her with such underhanded scandalous means would not be favourable to an agreeable or pleasurable future. And after his first, enthralling taste of her lips, he decided if they were to have a future together it would be a pleasurable one, not one founded on regret and shame.

He tilted her chin and deepened the kiss, leaving no doubt as to the effect she had on him. The touch of her fingers, delightful and tentative, made him burn. He throbbed, wanted to lift her skirts and have her up against the ivy-covered trellis. Have her moan his name against his ear as her hot core clamped around him, draining him of his own release.

Royce pulled away, shocked at his own reactions and dishonourable thoughts about the woman. She stared up at him with glassy, lust-fogged eyes that gleamed in the dappled moonlight. "You should return to the ball before you're missed," he said.

Her pink tongue slipped out onto her bottom lip as if to tease him completely senseless. Stifling a growl, Royce stood and lifted her to her slippered feet, then set about removing the telling evidence she had been thoroughly kissed and manhandled by a rogue.

With gentle precision, he positioned a misplaced curl back within the bonds of a pin, the soft curl tempting him to bury his hands in her silken locks. She would look exquisite with her golden-red hair cascading about her shoulders. Or better yet, against his pillows, all mussed from his lovemaking.

She slapped his hand away and stepped back. "I am perfectly able to right my dress and appearance, my lord."

"Of course, Miss March," he said unable to hide the smile in his voice.

"I suppose a gentleman of your reputation thinks of such trysts as normal and commonplace, certainly something to laugh about."

"On the contrary, Miss March, and if I have offended you, please accept my most humble apologies." Royce bit back a smile. She was a delightful minx to behold, feathers ruffled and indignant. A twinge pricked in his chest and he frowned.

She curtsied. "Good night, Lord Danning."

Royce clasped her fingers before she could stalk away and didn't miss the slight tremble that thrummed against his palm. "Good night, Miss March." The urge to kiss her again nearly overrode his control, but the defiant gleam in her eye told him she'd not take well to more kisses from him this eve, even upon her hand.

Still, plenty of other eves in the season.

Royce watched her walk toward the terrace doors, her skirts billowing about long, striding legs, leaving him in the shadows with desires that ran as hot as the Arabian desert during the midday sun. Miss March had always been delectable. Now, she was desirable.

<hr />

Later that night, Royce watched Suzanna waltz gracefully with Lord Moyle and a simmering anger he thought never to feel started to burn in his gut. Grudgingly, he acknowledged the nuance for what it was. Jealousy.

"May I grant you my heartfelt condolences, Lord Danning?"

Royce beat back the urge to snarl at Suzanna's brother.

"What do you mean, March?" He took a swig of his brandy, welcoming the distraction of the burn from his growing temper. How dare this bastard speak to him after the trouble he'd caused with his own fool of a sibling.

"As I understand it, you will soon be married." March smirked and looked out over the gathered throng of guests.

Royce frowned. "So the banns have been read? Comical. I hadn't thought I'd asked a woman to be my bride." He clenched his jaw at the resounding chuckle, which grated on his already frayed nerves.

"Well of course you will, my lord. A ruined viscount must marry, and soon. I should imagine you have your sights set on someone…wealthy?"

Equal to his own height, Royce glared into March's eyes, one burning question fogging his mind: how had the bastard found out his situation was so desperate? "Not unlike yourself, a grandson of a farmer trying to marry an earl's daughter. Do not think yourself so much different, March. At least I have no need to climb the social ladder, only to keep what is rightfully mine from birth." Royce inwardly cringed as Suzanna's words stabbed at his conscience. Perhaps he was too high in the instep.

March paused. "*Touché.* And you may do whatever you wish as long as the woman you seek is not my sister."

With a will of their own, Royce's gaze sought out the beautiful Miss March. She shone like the brightest candle flame in a room full of superbly gowned women. A rare light and one to be treasured.

Suzanna laughed at something Lord Moyle said, and a pang of regret pierced Royce's chest. She had once looked at him in such a way, with easy joviality before his hasty, hurtful words had sent her from London and travel abroad. And all because of his brother, and this arse standing next to him who couldn't control their gambling.

Yet they could not entirely be blamed for the family woes. Royce, as head of the family, had not been as careful as one should.

Yet not all was lost. Suzanna had kissed him, after all; perhaps there was hope for them still. He turned his attention back to Henry March. "Would such a decision not be up to Miss March? She is of age, is she not?"

The deadly gleam that entered March's eyes gave Royce an odd sense of pleasure. Annoying the bastard calmed the raging beast inside him that wanted to beat the cocky gentleman to a pulp.

"Seek her out for her fortune, and there will be hell to pay, Danning. Your treatment of her last year was uncalled for and nearly ruined her in the eyes of society. I would see her married to a man she loves and to one who will love her in return. Do I make myself clear?"

Royce chuckled. "And if I love her, will my suit then be welcome?"

"An easy gesture, to profess love to a rich lady when you are broke. You made it obvious she was not acceptable last season. Need I remind you my father established business in textile trading and finance? He worked his way to the wealth and position we hold in society. Or has her fortune blinded you to our common heritage?"

Royce looked away from Suzanna and inhaled a calming breath. "I have not forgotten. But I believe you have also overlooked the fact your sister had a tendre for me, one I wish restored. Keep an eye on her, March; my rakish wiles may see her wedded and bedded before the month is out." He smirked.

"Watch your mouth lest you find yourself wed and dead," March said, with a pointed stare before storming away.

Royce watched March go, and sighed. How he

regretted his words to Suzanna all those months ago. Hated to see her esteem for him wither and die with every hurtful word he'd uttered. His temper, having been spiked by his wayward brother, had been unfairly released on an innocent woman—one who would take much persuasion to believe he meant no harm by his words. It was probably for the best if he left her alone. Just then Suzanna laughed —a warm, wondrous sound—that sent fire coursing toward his groin. Impossible notion, and one he knew he wouldn't adhere to.

Royce looked away and caught sight of his friend, Lord Renn. The Earl waved and strode over.

"Danning, my good man, how have you been? It seems an age since I saw you last."

He scoffed. "If I recall the last time I saw you, Renn, you were disappearing from a ballroom with the married hostess. Who by the way," he said, nodding toward a group of ladies, "is looking in your direction."

Renn laughed. "It was a good night if I remember."

Royce raised an eyebrow at Renn's ignorance to his sarcasm. He shook his head. "What brings you to town? I thought you were for the continent this season?"

"I was. Made it all the way to Spain, then turned for home. Problem with my prized mare. Seems she's fallen pregnant and will not be racing this year after all."

Royce knew very well about prized mares. His gaze sought out Miss March. "Perhaps her foal will be your next great galloper."

Renn snorted. "Highly doubtful when its sire has a tendency for laziness during a race." He took a sip of his drink. "Saw you dancing with Miss March and having a cosy *tête-à-tête* with her brother. Care to enlighten an old friend?"

Royce stifled a growl over the reminder. "March was merely warning me off his sister."

Renn sputtered and choked on his drink. "Like you could possibly be interested in such a disaster. Do you remember last year when she spilt her champagne down the front of her white dress at the Dupree's garden party? But for all her awkwardness, she did have a lovely *décolletage*."

Royce clamped his hands into fists. The last thing he needed to do was lose his temper and come to blows with his best friend before the *ton*. He took a deep calming breath. "I would suggest you forget about Miss March and her awkward first season. I would also recommend your low opinion on Miss March be kept to yourself."

Renn looked at him with astonishment. "You're courting the disaster?"

Anger surged through Royce, and he turned a menacing glare on his soon-to-be ex-friend. "One more word against Miss March, and we are no longer acquaintances," he said, barely controlling his temper. "I wronged her last year and wish to make amends. I've always admired her person. It is just unfortunate she cannot choose her relatives."

"Yes, what a ghastly family. They stink of trade. Why, before her father died I swear he would arrive at entertainments covered in ink." Royce laughed. "I'm surprised Miss March can attend any balls and hold her head up high."

Royce watched Suzanna make her way back to her sibling, her easy graceful movement sure and confident. Last season she would have tripped over her own feet by now and would probably have been trying to stand without showing her ankles. Royce reluctantly admired her transformation into a graceful butterfly. She was a remarkable woman to grace the high sticklers of the *ton* and face them square on. Last season she could barely muster a word without stuttering but not anymore. "I suggest you leave, Renn. Now."

Renn frowned. "Apologies, Danning. I did not know your intentions toward the girl had changed." He cleared his throat. "Do not take offense, old man; who is to look out for you if not I. I am your oldest and best friend. One who, I believe, has the right to remind you the Dannings do not marry those without a title."

"Her brother's a gentleman," Royce said, not bothering to mask his menacing tone. "She is then worthy of my hand by your values."

Renn held his hands up in defeat. "All I meant was the people from trade are different from us. I do not want you to regret a decision you cannot easily mend. I mean, get hold of yourself, Danning; her grandfather was a farmer and not even a gentleman farmer!"

Royce gave his friend a hard look and refused to answer the man's spiteful and lofty principles. He let the taut silence stretch between them.

"Will we see you at Ascot this year?" Renn asked at length.

"No." Royce glared at March across the crowded ballroom, one of the men responsible for his missing the meet. The weight of the debt he owed settled on his shoulders and threatened to crumble him to his knees. "Not this year I'm afraid." Royce pushed the disappointment aside. Such circumstances were wont to happen when one was broke. He should probably start getting used to it.

"Probably a wise move. I hear Jannette is odds-on favourite of winning the Gold Cup. Next year perhaps." Renn signalled to an acquaintance across the room. "I'm off then. Good luck with Miss March or with whatever takes your fancy."

Royce glared at Renn's retreating as he walked away. He didn't appreciate being reminded of her lineage. Lineage that, should his parents still be alive, would never have suited. Yet Suzanna intrigued him. Had done so since the first night he saw her across the room last season, trying to hide behind her aunt and an abundance of fernery. She was sweet but with a strength of character that suited him. All he had to do now was convince her of this fact and see where it took them. Maybe all the way down a church aisle.

※

"Lost in thought?" her brother asked Suzanna as he came to stand at her side, Victoria clasping his arm.

Suzanna pulled her mind away from the past. "Yes, you could say that."

"Why was Lord Danning sniffing about your skirts?"

"Henry," she admonished. "You should know better than anyone. Lord Danning would not go sniffing about *my* skirts."

"He might with the newly improved Suzanna who now graces the *ton* and lights up every room."

Suzanna slapped her brother's arm with her fan. "Don't be such a tease. His lordship cares for me as much as I care for him, which is naught. He was merely being polite, I imagine."

Her gaze sought Lord Danning, who was bending to talk to a dark-haired beauty in a deep blue gown. "See," she gestured toward his lordship, "he's already found what he sought. I was merely a host's duty and unable to be ignored."

"You would be hard to ignore, Suzanna."

"Thank you, Victoria, you're a dear friend." She swallowed the lump in her throat at the sight of Lord Danning taking the woman out to dance. It was silly, really. Kisses like the one he bestowed were granted, no doubt, many times to other women. To think she had seen or felt anything further in his actions other than lust and need was a notion she should throw to the wind.

"Are you sure he was so very mean last season? Perhaps you caught him at an unfortunate moment."

"Suzanna will not be marrying Viscount Danning, no matter his past or future intentions toward her."

"Why do you hate him so much, Henry?" Suzanna boldly asked. Never had she heard such hatred in her brother's tone.

"I think what he said to you last year is reason enough." He waved the comment away. "In any case, be assured I will not approve of such a choice and would recommend you look elsewhere for a husband."

"First of all, I was never looking at Danning as a suitable candidate in the first place. He spoke to me, and I ended the conversation as quickly as it started. Do not worry yourself over a possibility that will never occur."

"I lost sight of you for a time." Her brother gave her a pointed stare. "Tell me you did not step out with him. You know he's a rake and would probably welcome ruining you now that he realizes the atrocious way he spoke to you last season didn't kill you stone dead in the *ton*."

"Don't be absurd. Lord Danning, for all his politeness —or lack thereof—has not done me any damage this eve." *Besides kissing her senseless.*

Victoria looked at her with narrowed eyes before she turned toward the dancing couples. "I see he's dancing with Lady Flintstock, an heiress from Cumberland, I believe," she said with a consoling smile.

"Yes, a thorough and pure lady with a title that stretches back to Queen Elizabeth." Suzanna sighed.

"She has a rather pinched face, though, don't you agree?" her brother asked, one eyebrow raised.

Suzanna frowned. "Henry you should know better than to be so insensitive. At least she's not tarnished."

"You are not tarnished, Suzanna. Unless there is something you are not telling me." Henry met her gaze.

"No," she said, clasping her brother's arm, and hoping a blush, over what she'd done earlier, didn't bloom on her cheeks. "I only meant we are tarnished...by trade."

"Oh, of course, how could I forget." Her brother laughed. "But better that, my dear, than tarnished by debt."

CHAPTER 5

"Lady Victoria to see you, Miss Suzanna."

Suzanna looked up from her latest *La Belle Assemblée*, and noted the time. "Tea, please, Peter and have cook plate up some macaroons. I know they're one of Lady Victoria's favourites."

"Yes, miss." The butler dipped his head and departed. A smile quirked her lips at the sound of Victoria's slippered feet patting across the parquetry foyer floor. She was a loyal and wonderful friend, and after the questioning look Victoria had bestowed on her at the ball last week, Suzanna had been waiting for her to call.

"Beautiful weather we're having, Suzanna," Victoria said, coming toward her and kissing her cheeks. "Perhaps tomorrow we could persuade Henry to take us out in the carriage, perhaps a turnabout Hyde Park? What do you say?"

"Sounds like a marvellous idea. I'm sure Henry would agree."

They sat on the settee before the unlit hearth. Victoria pulled her gloves off and placed them on the table, then turned to her. A knowing silence stretched between them.

With a resounding sigh, Victoria spoke. "At the ball last week, I saw you step out with Lord Danning and not reappear until sometime later. What were you up to?"

"Nothing of consequence." Suzanna paused, her mind a whir of excuses. "He apologized for his treatment and harsh words last season. That was all."

"Why are you blushing then? I am your dearest and best friend, so please tell me. I would never dishonour you by telling anyone else, if that is your concern."

Suzanna slumped back into the settee. The overwhelming urge to confide in her friend was too much to resist. "He kissed me. Well, actually, we seemed to kiss each other at the same time. One moment, we were arguing and then the next I had an urge to show him what he threw away." Suzanna touched her lips remembering the feel of him, his ardent mouth, and his roaming hands that sent shivers down her spine even now. Her cheeks burned.

"You kissed Lord Danning! Oh my." Victoria made a play of fanning herself. "What was it like?"

Suzanna smiled. "Marvellous. His lips were quite energetic and able. But then.... He did the oddest thing and used his tongue. It was most interesting and made my stomach feel as if butterflies were taking flight within."

"That does sound marvellous but a little strange. Will you be doing it again, do you think?" Victoria's eyes were wide with excitement.

"No." Suzanna frowned, as her answer brought forth a deep emptiness inside. "Well, perhaps if he bestows such liberties again on me. You know I could never initiate such wantonness myself."

"Why do you think he kissed you? After his words last season...."

It was a question Suzanna had been asking herself. Perhaps Lord Danning was sorry for his rudeness and really wished to make amends. And being a rake of the highest calibre, perhaps kissing innocent women was his way of making it up to them.

"I'm not entirely sure," she answered in all honesty. "Perchance he is truly sorry. He certainly seemed sincere."

Victoria chuckled and rose from her seat, pacing before the hearth. "I think you should play a little game with Lord Danning. He was rude and uncouth last year to be sure and now he should pay a penalty for his behaviour. I think," Victoria pulled Suzanna to her feet, "that you should dangle yourself before him, make him realize what he has thrown away, and can no longer have. Tease him shamelessly."

Suzanna stilled, hearing a plan she herself had thought to accomplish the eve of the kiss; before Lord Danning and his wicked lips had taken her senses and decorum and thrown them into the cesspit of loose morals and gentlemanly needs.

"Are you telling me, Victoria, you think I should kiss him again? That such behaviour would be something with which you concur when a woman's been slighted as I?"

Her friend grinned and nodded. "That is exactly what I think you should do. It's about time we women stood up for ourselves and were no longer seen as a commodity to be bought when a gentleman has tired of his latest *chère-amie*."

"This is such a wicked plan." Suzanna paused. "His kisses were very nice, but what shall I do if he tries to take my favours further?"

"You are a sensible woman. I know you'll not allow it to proceed too far. And then when the season ends and you receive a proposal from Lord Danning, you may give him his *congé* and marry someone else. And serves him right, too," Victoria said with a decisive nod.

The thought of the proud Lord Danning heartbroken and at Suzanna's feet, tears running down his strong, unshaven jaw.... No, such an image didn't suit him at all. She shook the reflection away. He'd more than likely shrug and head to Whites for a game of cards and a glass of their finest brandy.

"Very well, I'll dangle myself before him like a ripe mouse before a cat and we'll see if he walks into my trap. What do I have to lose?"

"Well, your reputation, my dear, should anyone find out about the game you're playing with Lord Danning. You must be discreet, that is foremost important. Yet you should also make him believe he could receive further favours from you other than kissing, yet never in reality. Oh, this will be such fun. You must promise to keep me informed," Victoria begged, clasping her hands, only restraining her excitement when a footman brought in the tea tray. Her friend's eyes lit up when she spied the macaroons. "Oh, you're a dearest, Suzanna. You know how much I love macaroons."

Suzanna laughed, poured the tea, and ensured Victoria had an ample serving of her favourite sweet. "So where do you think I should start my plan of seduction?"

"Oh yes, *seduction* is just the right word to use," Victoria said, her gaze bright with mischief and the crumbs of her macaroon speckling her lips. "The Staffon's ball is three days away. Lord Danning is sure to be there, as will you."

"Yes, Aunt Agnes has already started to worry about the engagement. You know how she is in such company." Suzanna bit into a macaroon and wondered how her aunt would handle one of the biggest events of this season.

"Mama will be attending with me; and she will keep your aunt company. Do not worry, Suzanna."

"Thank you, Victoria, you're a true friend."

"That I am, my dearest. One who is determined to see you marry well while at the same time bring the high and mighty Lord Danning to his knees. He shall pine forever over the loss of you."

It was what Suzanna wanted as well as long as she did not encourage an entanglement ending in her ruination.

※

Three days later, Suzanna stood alone watching Lord Danning from across the room at the Staffon's ball. Unaware of her gaze, he moved through the *ton* like a predator stalking its next meal. Little did he know he was going to be hers.

Tonight, he wore a shadow across his jaw that made him seem more wild and roguish than normal. Given his reputation in the *ton* already, many a woman's head turned at the sight of him and Suzanna was no different. She couldn't look away from him. He might not be easy to seduce, but he would be worth the effort—she was sure.

One taste of him had proven that.

Dressed in white silk, Suzanna blended with the many white-clad women privileged with an invitation. Lady Staffon always stipulated her guests wear one colour of her choice to her balls, whereas the hostess was free to wear any colour she chose. Blue was her choice this evening with a gown that drew the eye of many a gentleman, and Lord Danning was no exception.

Suzanna frowned as his lordship's gaze lowered on the bountiful *décolletage* of the married hostess for longer than was deemed proper as if any time at all was deemed proper to view another lady's breasts. She gazed down at her own cleavage and wondered if there was enough there with which to tease him. Certainly, the other night he had seemed pleased with her person. The rake obviously had some sort of tendre for that part of a woman's anatomy.

How strange....

"You look beautiful, Suzanna. Do not worry; as soon as Lord Danning sees you, my dear, he will make his way over. Why, you've already danced with many a gentleman, enough to cause even our hostess to become a little jealous."

"He has not noticed me yet." Suzanna met Victoria's gaze and raised her brows. "Perhaps a plan of seduction was wishful thinking on my part."

"Nonsense. He has only just arrived. Give him time." Her friend paused and took a sip of her champagne. "Is your brother coming tonight?"

"No. He said he had a previous engagement." Suzanna looked out into the throng and met the heavy-lidded stare of Lord Danning leaning against the wall. She took in his fine skin-tight breeches that left nothing of what lay beneath to the imagination. Not to mention his wide shoulders and large hands...hands that had been against her body, pulling her close, and touching her with a reverence that still left her breathless.

"See, my dear. Here he comes."

So lost in her perusal of him, Suzanna hadn't noticed him walking their way. Oh dear, what would she say to the man? Now the time had come to play the siren, she wasn't at all sure she was capable of such antics. It was one thing to think she could do such things but quite another to actually do them.

She looked away from the delectable sight he made and watched the elderly Lord Bromley dance with his wife, thirty years his junior. A disturbing sight, sure to pull one's mind away from what was bearing down on her with belly-tensing speed.

"Good evening, Lady Victoria, Miss March," Lord Danning said with a slight bow. Suzanna curtsied and took in his smouldering eyes. Embarrassment swamped her when she realized his gaze was not directed at her but her friend.

"Good evening, Lord Danning." Victoria glanced her way, before looking back to his lordship. "Are you enjoying the ball, my lord?"

"I am, my lady and ever more so now that I may have the delightful pleasure of dancing with you."

A flush rose on her friends cheeks. "Oh, I hadn't thought to dance tonight, my lord."

At Victoria's attempt to dissuade Lord Danning, Suzanna took pity on her friend and the awkward silence that settled about them all. "You should enjoy the evening. I'll find your mama and sit with her."

"Are you sure? I don't wish to leave you alone." Victoria frowned.

Suzanna quickly met Lord Danning's eyes and smiled. The gesture was all she could summon due to the lump wedged in her throat. "Of course," she said quickly. "In fact I've just spotted your mama. I will see you a little later." And with a quick curtsy, Suzanna moved toward the ballroom doors with no intention of seeking out Victoria's mama.

Cool air hit her face as she moved into the less crowded passageway, a welcome reprieve from the overcrowded stifling ballroom. She leaned against the wall and caught her breath that seemed to be coming in rapid repetition.

What a silly fool she was, to imagine Lord Danning would fall for her. A ridiculous notion she should never have contemplated. To think she had been going to seduce him and play him for a fool. Yet, once again he had trumped her ace. No, squashed her under his leather topboots like an annoying little ant not worth his notice. She had presented herself like a wanton hussy and heat stole up her neck at the thought. Not that she did anything terribly wrong. Yet one should never allow rakes to kiss them in the way he had last week in the garden.

Suzanna pushed away from the wall and ambled toward the retiring room. No one spoke to her when she made her way to a window seat overlooking the darkened garden and stared out at her reflection on the glass.

Perhaps being here, among the highest London peerage, was a foolish notion. Yet tonight she seemed popular with the gentlemen; but more than likely her acceptance this eve was solely due to arriving with Victoria's mama, the Countess of Ross.

The lump was back in her throat and tears welled. She wiped them away and sniffed. What lunacy to think she could find a husband in this society. Yes, she had wealth but what of it when no one cared about nor welcomed such a family into their lives.

She needed a change of scenery.

No longer would she refuse the abundant cards of the lower society that arrived daily and sat unopened on her brother's desk. At least by marrying a gentleman from her own sphere, her chances of marrying for love and not for some Lord's financial gain were in her favour.

Calm settled about her like a comforting hug. It was the right decision, a decision long overdue.

The *ton* could go hang.

R oyce stood at the side of the Tattersall's auction ring and fought not to lose his decorum. All morning the auctioneer slammed down the hammer like a death knell on his prized horseflesh and vehicles. With every item sold, Royce cursed himself and his brother to Hades.

His friend, Lord Renn, was even here, purchasing his prized horseflesh without a flicker of remorse. Self-disgust ate at him, the feeling lying heavily on his shoulders.

It was a sobering day.

"With the horse sales, the harvest reaping, and the sale of your Rome estate, I do believe you'll see your financial situation to rights, my lord."

Royce glanced at his solicitor tallying away in his notebook. He cringed as the final hammer gong came down on his champion two-year old, Kingstar. There went his racing season. His temper soared when the even-tempered colt was led from the arena by Suzanna's brother, Mr. Henry March.

"Bastard."

"Pardon, my lord?" His solicitor gazed at him in concern.

"Nothing." Royce marched over to the auctioneer and thanked him for his services before returning to his man of business. "Pay off the most pressing debts immediately, and send word to me of who is left to pay. Write to them and see if they will hold off until the harvest is in. It is not too much to ask, surely." Royce could only hope the debtors agreed.

"Yes, my lord." His solicitor nodded and sauntered toward his carriage. Royce walked out onto the street and realized he no longer had the luxury of such a vehicle. Hailing a hackney cab, he jumped in and threw himself onto the squabs. The smell of tobacco and vomit wafted from the seat.

Royce shook his head and lowered the cab's window, disgusted by the odour that would ruin his suit. This would never do. How could he continue to grace society when all would be privy to him selling off his horses and carriages? To explain away such an action would be impossible. The *ton* would never believe the excuse he merely wished to renew his stock. They would see through his lie like a piece of glass.

Royce yelled out his direction to the driver and clasped the belt above the window as the carriage rumbled over the cobbled road. His thoughts turned to his brother whom he'd not seen these past four days.

He frowned.

CHAPTER 6

Over the following weeks, Suzanna attended many balls and parties of London's gentry' society. Henry, happy to see her away from the money-hungry rakes of the upper London *ton*, attended with her and made the necessary introductions when required.

It was very liberating, Suzanna found, to be the most sought after and highly regarded, among their set. The only drawback was Victoria's absence from her side. Being an earl's daughter, her friend circulated in a different sphere to the one Suzanna now called home.

"Penny for your thoughts, Suzanna."

With a sigh, she looked across at her brother seated in the family carriage. His eyes and his white cravat were the only parts she could make out of him in the darkened space. "Just a penny? You're turning cheap, Henry." At his resounding chuckle, Suzanna laughed. "I was just thinking of how much I miss Victoria and yet not her society at all."

"We are as good as anyone else." Henry shifted on his seat, a sign of his aggravation at the reminder of their heritage. "Our money may have come from the hard work of our father, but his fortune was honestly earned and not to be considered lightly. I wager, had a high and mighty lord needed your fortune desperately enough, his dearest mama would have been easy enough to buy. Makes me sick, thinking of you marrying a rogue who is only after your purse. To risk having you thrust into a family who, after access to your blunt, may have treated you abominably."

Suzanna sighed, one rogue in particular coming to mind although Lord Danning had no need for her money. What a shame he didn't attend some of the balls of her new sphere. He would then see what a catch she was, even if not to his taste.

"I understand Mr. Jenkins will be in attendance this evening."

"Really," Suzanna said, trying to hide the boredom that entered her voice at the mention of the man. A baron's third son who thought she would make him a perfect wife, whether affection was involved or not. Not in her case.

Had she not escaped to her brother's side two evenings past, Suzanna was sure she'd still be trapped in Mrs. Hill's supper room, listening to him preach about the appalling gravel paths in Hyde Park and how he'd tripped over a pebble some days past. Pity the boring man wouldn't fall into the Serpentine and disappear altogether. "How fortunate for us," she said.

Henry grinned. "So you won't be marrying the poor fellow, then?"

"Certainly not." Suzanna met her brother's laughing gaze. "And I expect if he comes to call, you will let him down gently and save him the embarrassment of hearing it from me."

"I will do no such thing, Suzanna. If he asks, you will

do your duty and tell him *no* yourself. In any case," he said, checking his cravat and picking up his hat, "you should be warned, it is not only Mr. Jenkins who's been looking at you for a wife. Many gentlemen have approached me and asked of you. Surely one of them meets your favour?"

"Not yet," she said, clasping the seat as the carriage rocked to a halt. "But I'll let you know when one does."

"Marvellous." Henry's reply cloaked in sarcasm. "Now come; dinner awaits."

Suzanna entered the foyer of Baronet Blyth's Belgravia home. With the help of a footman, she shrugged off her cloak and took her brother's arm. Sir William and his wife, Lady Blyth, greeted them warmly at the drawing room door before ushering them inside. Footmen bustled about, serving hors d'oeuvres and drinks to the gathered throng. Suzanna glanced about the room to see who was present. Her steps faltered.

"He's a cad," her brother growled through his teeth. "If he thinks I'll give you away to him, he has rocks in his head."

Suzanna patted his arm and smiled as they came up to a group of ladies of her acquaintance. "I'm sure he has a reason for being present. I highly doubt it's because of me."

"Suzanna," he said, pulling her to a stop. "You would make a most suitable and equal wife to Viscount Danning. And he knows it. I've no doubt he is here because of you. Tell me," he paused, looking over her shoulder, his eyes narrowing in the direction of his lordship, "have you ever seen him in this society before?"

She frowned and shook her head. "No."

"Neither have I. But the moment you step away from the *ton*, he comes crawling into our sphere like a dog sniffing out a wealthy bone."

"Don't be so rude, Henry. Lord Danning, for whatever

reason, is here as a guest of Sir Blyth. You must be polite or I'll tell Victoria what a grouch of a husband you will make." Suzanna chuckled at the blush that rose on her brother's cheeks.

"You're a cruel woman, Suzanna."

She smiled and pulled him toward her new friends. "Not cruel at all and you know it. Just making sure you behave like the gentleman I know you to be."

Sometime later, Henry escorted her into dinner where, much to Suzanna's despair, she was deposited beside Lord Danning. Henry, seated across from her, threw his lordship a baleful glare before turning to the entree before him.

"So this is where you have been hiding over the last few weeks, Miss March." Lord Danning looked about the room with a studied air.

"I thought a change of society would do me well, my lord, and up until this eve it had done so." He smiled and Suzanna immediately regretted her politely worded set down. Having told her brother to act the gentleman, she had been unable to hold her own tongue.

"Lady Victoria misses you greatly, I believe. Will you ever come back and light up our ballrooms as you once did?"

A spike of irrational jealousy shot through her at the thought of Victoria airing her feelings to Lord Danning and receiving condolences in return. It was silly of her; Lord Danning could speak with whomever he wished; she was nothing to him. And Victoria was her friend and she should not think ill of her over a man. Especially this man. "I saw Victoria only last week, my lord. I do believe you are exaggerating."

"On the contrary, Miss March. Why, only last eve while dancing a waltz with her she told me how she wished you were there. Of course, I concurred and said I would take it upon myself to find out where you had gone and what you find so favourable to keep you away."

Barely repressing her temper, Suzanna placed down her spoon and turned toward the vexing man at her side. "Well, now you have found me. Do not let me be the one to hold you from your entertainments. You see, I happen to like this society and the people who grace it. As for the last sphere I graced, other than Victoria, I cannot say there was anything else to recommend it."

Lord Danning clasped his chest. "You wound my fragile heart."

Her eyes narrowed and she took a calming breath. "What are you really doing here, Lord Danning?"

He smiled and sipped his wine. "I've come to see you. I've missed you."

"Really?" Suzanna chuckled, the sound tinged with sarcasm. "You're a liar and a rogue, my lord. And if you think I will fall for your pretty words, you're sadly mistaken."

He grinned. "Has anyone ever told you how beautiful you are when you're angry? Your temper suits the fiery colour of your hair."

Suzanna looked about the table in fear of others hearing his lordship's inappropriate compliment. She shushed him. "Perhaps you should heed the warning my hair is giving you then, my lord. And in any case, you're wasting your flattery on me." The feel of satin knee breeches, a knee in particular, rubbed suggestively against her leg. Suzanna struggled to swallow her mouthful of soup as her breath caught in her lungs. Her body longed to feel the man beside her and she quickly squashed the emotion like a bug.

"In all honesty, I came because Sir Blyth is one of my

oldest and dearest friends. We attended Cambridge together."

Suzanna swallowed and met Lord Danning's eye before looking about the table. She had not known he had such a friendship with Sir Blyth. It would explain the genial banter between the two before dinner. To know he did not decry the middle aristocratic class placed him in a slightly more favourable light.

Only slightly.

"You're surprised?" he asked, mirth visible in his dark-blue orbs.

Suzanna shrugged. "Of course I am, my lord. I wouldn't have thought," she said in a lowered voice, "Sir Blyth was deemed good *ton*."

"He isn't, by high society's standards but by mine, of course."

He smiled as the first course was cleared from before them. His appreciative study of her made her stomach somersault, reminding her of the night they were together on the terrace....

"You shouldn't look at me like so, my lord. It's disconcerting."

He chuckled but said nothing. Nor did he need for Suzanna to know what he was thinking. The very same thoughts as she was having. Of them locked together under an ivy vine, his hands against her flesh, holding her captive to an onslaught of desire, which until that night was unknown to her.

Suzanna reached for her water and fumbling, spilled the entire drink on the white, highly starched tablecloth. Heat bloomed on her face and as she stood to avoid the liquid spilling onto her skirt, she heard a resounding thud —her chair crashing against the floorboards.

"I'm so sorry, Sir Blyth. I'm so clumsy." Unable to still

the tremor running though her hands, Suzanna tried to mop up the abundant spill with her napkin.

Sir Blyth waved her concerns away and summoned a footman. "Please see to the mess, and fetch Miss March another glass of water."

Suzanna slumped onto her chair and when she sat into nothing but thin air, wished the ground would open up and swallow her whole. All the humiliations of last season came crashing down, along with the remains of her dinner, when her hands shot out to clasp anything to stop her fall.

Shouts and gasps sounded about her. Suzanna looked down at her ruined gown, covered in the *entrée*. The multi-coloured stain also covered most of her bosom.

Unable to stop herself, she looked up at Lord Danning, whose visage was impossible to read. She pushed away his offer of help and gained her feet, striding from the room with all the dignity she could muster, willing her feet to take her far from the scene of such complete humiliation. All those months and money spent on making her a lady who fit the *ton* and all its lofty ideals were for nothing. She had not changed; she was still the unlucky debutante from last season.

At the sound of voices and footsteps from behind, Suzanna rushed down the hallway and fled into the ladies retiring room. She shut the door and leaned against it in the hopes whoever had followed her would be discouraged and leave her alone. When the door opened with an almighty shove, she was thrown face down onto the Aubusson rug. It seemed such a wish was not to be granted this eve.

. . .

"Suzanna, I do apologize. Here," Royce said, leaning down and pulling her to stand. "I would never have barged in had I known you were standing behind the door." He watched her right her clothes as best she could before she turned, sauntered over to a basin of water, and tried to wipe the remains of her dinner from her gown.

Suzanna glared at him over her shoulder as a blob of sauce dropped and splattered onto the floor. "My clothes are already soiled, so landing on the floor for a second time this evening will not matter."

His gaze stole over her ruined apparel and the sad, unsure woman he had known last year stared back at him across the room. An ache settled in his chest at the dishevelled picture she made. All of which was his fault. Had he not tried to fluster her by touching her leg, she would not have suffered such humiliation.

"I apologize if my actions earlier this night upset you to the point you spilled—"

"My drink. All over the table before falling on my backside in front of the dinner guests I was trying to impress. Since," she walked over to him and poked his chest with a finger, "the society I had initially graced wanted naught to do with me and all because of a certain pompous, arrogant, high-in-the-instep lord."

Royce sighed. Her tone did not bode well for his plan to win Suzanna and make her his wife. "Like I said, I apologize. Perhaps for me to make amends, you would agree to a ride in the park tomorrow. I believe the weather is to be congenial."

"Unlike the company," she stated, with a narrow, piercing stare that could have turned him to ash on the Aubusson rug beneath his boots.

"There's no need to be…." Her eyes narrowed further

as Royce cut off what he was about to say. He doubted his suggestion that she should be polite would place her in a more pleasant mood.

"You should leave, my lord. If you could find my brother and send him in, I would be appreciative."

Royce tucked a flyaway curl behind her ear and noted for the first time a delightful mole above her slightly parted and lusciously plump lip. She was mouth-watering in this dishevelled state. A little of the soup clung to a strand of her hair, and he had an overwhelming urge to clean it away. She pulled away from his hand.

"And you may stop looking at me like that, Lord Danning." She ambled toward the window and fumbled with the heavy velvet drapes drawn closed for the evening. "I know I may make interesting sport for a rake of the *ton*, but I refuse to allow you to laugh at my clumsiness or make me cry any longer. I want you to leave."

Royce watched her attempt to hold her composure and a fear unlike any he had ever known assailed him. He'd made her cry?

"Suzanna, don't be upset." He took a step toward her.

"How can I not be upset? You purposefully toyed with me at dinner, to the point where I again became that clumsy freckled redheaded girl who hails from trade with not an ounce of breeding or the decorum to suit your exalted sphere. You made the society in which I belong scorn me."

"They would not think such a thing, especially Sir and Lady Blyth. Two people I hold in high regard."

"Of course, you would say such a thing. You're a Viscount, lord of all you survey. They would not dare naysay or slight you."

"You're wrong," Royce said, unable to believe the venomous tone of Suzanna's words.

"Am I? I'm not so sure." She turned from the window, and Royce noted her glassy, bright eyes. She started for the exit and he knew he couldn't let her go, believing what she said. Royce stepped in front of the door and refused to permit her to leave.

"Get out of my way."

"I cannot. I've made you cry. Please, Suzanna, don't be angry or distressed at my foolish attempt to seduce you. I never meant you harm."

She glared at him for what seemed an age, the dislike in her green depths as murky as the sea. Then the crack of her hand slapping his skin echoed loudly in the room. Royce stood still, shocked to his core. Never had he been slapped by a person in his entire life. Not even his stern father had laid a hand against him during his childhood. And God knows he'd deserved it at times. The experience was quite...novel, even if it did sting like the blazes.

"Why did you do that?"

"Move, or I'll do it again. You deserved it, you cad."

She tried to move about him, and he clasped her arms to hold her still. Her skin, the colour of alabaster, was soft under his hands. Her upper arms were so slight he was able to wrap his hands fully about them. "I am not a cad. I may have certain rakish wiles but I'm not a cad." At her shocked gasp over his words, he frowned. "Why don't you like me?"

"I've already told you why, Lord Danning. There is nothing more to be said on the subject."

Royce thought there was plenty yet to say but her upturned nose indicated she was ignoring him. "Miss Suzanna March, if you are so determined to leave me to this ladies retiring room, would you allow me one wish?"

"I certainly will not." Suzanna met his gaze and then quickly looked away.

"Suzanna, may I kiss you goodnight?"

Her eyes widened and Royce seized the opportunity her shocked countenance afforded him. He took her lips and again, he was shocked at how sweet and innocent they tasted, a heady mixture that sent his senses reeling and his body longing for more. She opened for him, sighing into his mouth at their joining.

He walked her until the retiring room door stood at her back. Using the doors support, he lifted her leg a little to sit against his hip. Her body beneath the fine silk gown was perfection, and he reveled in the feel of her soft skin. How he'd love to pull the stockings from her long legs with his teeth, to taste and conquer the delicacies that awaited him between her legs.

She gasped at their closeness, his breathing as ragged as hers. His cock stood to attention and he rubbed it against her sex, pulling back a little to watch as her emerald eyes opened in awe.

Moving, he teased them both, her hands spiking through his hair to bring his lips back to hers, kissing *him* this time, and leaving him in unknown waters he'd never sailed before, where emotions ran riot, and need overtook want.

His hand strayed to her ass and he felt the moment her propriety pulled her back from the brink of pleasure. She pushed him away, striding toward a small writing desk on the opposite side of the room.

"Why do you always use seduction as a means to coerce? I'm not a toy to be messed about and thrown away when I'm no longer fun. I am so angry at you I could throw this paperweight at your head. And I certainly should never have kissed you."

Royce rubbed his jaw. "My apologies, Suzanna. Truly. It is just whenever I'm in your presence I cannot help myself. I like you. I like you very much." He sighed and walked toward her. Suzanna's gaze was wary, yet she did not move away. "I've always thought you a beautiful woman. You are kind and gentle, not a common affection found in the *ton*." He clasped her gloved hand and was thankful she did not pull it away. "You are a lady of the first water who I would like to know better."

Her eyes bored into his as if to try and seek the lie she was sure he told. She would find none; what he spoke was the truth.

"You were so rude to me last season. You cut me stone dead in the ballroom before so many people. Why did you do it? I thought we were friends."

Royce pulled her toward a settee and sat. "It wasn't you I was mad at. You found me at an unfortunate moment. My behaviour was not gentlemanly, and I apologize for the pain I caused you. I never meant to hurt you, or make you believe I thought you beneath me because of your family connections."

"What was so wrong that you reacted in such a way with me?"

Royce frowned. The last thing he wanted Suzanna to know was her brother had been the cause of his ill humour and part of the reason for his family's financial strife. The inability of both of their brothers to cease gambling and wasting time in the dens of London had caused him to snap at her. Hurt her.

He met her gaze and swallowed the lump of a lie which threatened to choke him. To tell her the truth now could ruin the delicate truce they'd seemed to form in the last few minutes. He couldn't risk losing her now, not through the fault of others. She did not need to be privy to his problems.

"It was a private matter I've since dealt with...or am dealing with, I should say. You mustn't concern yourself."

She smiled but something in her eyes told Royce she didn't wholly believe him. "So," he said, wanting to change the subject. "Will you ride with me tomorrow?"

"Where?"

"If you're in agreement, I'd like you to take the air with me around Hyde Park," he asked.

Suzanna eyed him for a moment then shrugged. "Why are you doing this, Lord Danning? Are we to be friends again, then?"

He nodded. "It is certainly something I wish." He paused. "And perhaps being seen with me may help you gain favour back in the *ton* should I have damaged it in any way in the past." The *ton* could go hang itself as far as Royce cared but it seemed to be something important to Suzanna, and if it persuaded her to join him on an outing he was clever enough to use the ruse.

She stared at him and her dishevelled state made her look uncommonly pretty. Unable to deny himself, Royce lent in and kissed her in a quick embrace he wished could go on forever. He pulled back and stared at Suzanna as his body roared with need, bucked at its denial of her, yet something more also simmered under his skin. A need to protect. To care.

"I suppose I could." Suzanna stood and walked to the door. Royce took the opportunity to watch her hips sway in an unconscious seduction. He tore his gaze from her derriere.

"I'll be ready at five o'clock. Don't be late," Suzanna added.

He stood, and bowed. "Until tomorrow, Miss March."

"Good night, my lord."

CHAPTER 7

"You are not stepping outside this house in the company of that rogue."

Suzanna gritted her teeth against her brother's dictate, one she intended to ignore. "You may be my brother, but Lord Danning is an eligible gentleman and one with whom I choose to associate."

"Why would you want to step out with a man who only last year caused you so much heartache? Don't try and fool me into believing he wasn't the reason you hightailed it to Paris." Henry slumped into the chair behind his desk and ran a hand over his face. "Explain to me why you would wish to do such a thing."

Suzanna frowned and wondered at her reasoning. Lord Danning had been cruel, but something urged her to give him a second chance. Had she not also, on occasion, snapped at the people she loved when out of sorts and in ill humour? "Lord Danning has apologized and explained our unfortunate interaction last season to my satisfaction. And let us not forget to be seen with a viscount could sway the *haute ton* to see me in a more favourable light, and not a lady covered in ink. I need to find a husband, Henry. I cannot live with you forever, not to mention Aunt Agnes is getting on in age."

"You say you are satisfied and believe this rubbish Viscount Danning spouts?"

"Of course," she said. "Why does that surprise you?"

"Because he's a money-hungry rogue only after your fortune, and he's in queer street up to his haughty eyebrows."

Suzanna ambled over to the window that looked out onto Curzon Street and watched polished carriages pass by, their wheels rumbling over the cobbled road. "You don't know that."

"I do and you will not marry him."

At her brother's stern expression, Suzanna smiled. "Of course I will not. I believe this carriage outing is only a means to apologize. No reason for you to go into a state of panic. I'll be back within the hour." At her statement, a highly polished curricle stopped before the house and excitement skittered across Suzanna's skin. "His lordship is here. I'll see you in an hour or so."

"Suzanna?"

"Yes?" she asked, stopping at the library door.

"You deserve a marriage of love, not one that will serve only to fill some rogue's coffers. He is after your money, my dear, no matter what sonnets or other pretty words he sings."

"I'm determined to marry for love, Henry, and I will. I'll not be drawn in, I promise you." She blew him a kiss and left, hoping her anticipation at seeing Lord Danning again was entirely platonic.

Yet knowing her eagerness was not.

"You look delightful, Miss March," Lord Danning said as he settled beside her on the bench. He picked up the ribbons and flicked them over the haunches of his two matched greys, which stood stomping in place.

"Thank you. Such flattery, my lord."

"It is no more than the truth." He grinned and her legs felt like jelly.

She tried to ignore the compliment and the heat flaming her cheeks by studying their surroundings. Carriages busy with afternoon trade pulled onto the roads around them, weaving through the traffic trying to gain their destination in the quickest possible time.

Lord Danning seemed unfazed and handled his pair with ease. Soon the gates of Hyde Park came into view and so, too, members of the *ton* taking the air this warm spring day.

"I believe Lady Victoria will be in the park. Do you wish to see her?"

"Of course," Suzanna said, a little dejected at the realization Lord Danning was keeping a record of her friend's whereabouts.

"I heard her mention it at a ball I attended after I left the dinner party last eve." He held her gaze. "I do not wish to court her."

Suzanna shrugged. "Why should you not court her? She is a woman of your station and of an age to marry. She would make you a very fine wife."

"I don't desire Lady Victoria as my bride, nor do I hold romantic inclinations towards her."

At the deep huskiness in his voice, Suzanna reminded herself she was there to be seen, not to start a flirtation with the viscount. She cleared her throat. "There are many people about today."

Lord Danning chuckled. "Yes, there are."

They drove for a time in quiet before, unable to stand the silence any longer, Suzanna inquired, "And have you any plans for this evening?"

"Yes, I am attending the Moncroft's masquerade."

"I do believe we were invited." Suzanna stifled a gasp as Lord Danning's thigh brushed hers and a bolt of awareness shot throughout her body. She shifted aside and fidgeted with her gloves, hoping he hadn't noticed her reaction to his closeness. After his kiss the other night, all she could think of was being so close again, of him touching her, devouring her in every delicious way.

"Well, you must attend." Lord Danning manoeuvred the carriage to the side of the path so another could pass before he turned to her, his dark eyes hooded with an emotion she could not name. "I would love to waltz with you, Miss March."

"Suzanna, please, my lord. Miss March can sound so droll at times."

He laughed, and another shiver of delight stole over her body. Why did his voice make her react in such a way? "You do understand I view our newfound friendship as just a friendship, my lord?"

He smiled and looked away. "If it is what you wish, then of course I'll honour your wishes."

Suzanna gazed at his lordship and noted her words had somehow stripped warmth from his gaze. At the sound of laughter, she looked toward a copse of trees and saw Victoria walking some distance before her mama's carriage with a gentleman Suzanna did not recognize.

"That is Mr. Swinson, an American from New York. He's rich as Croesus and only too eager to publicize the fact."

"By the tone of your voice I gather you do not like the gentleman, my lord?"

"No, I do not. He's a gambler."

Suzanna frowned at the hateful tone of Lord Danning's words. "You do not approve of gamblers or the vice?"

"Not at all, but to lose one's fortune and estates which generations before you have worked hard to keep," he said, meeting her gaze, "is the worst kind of treachery."

"I agree," Suzanna said. "Seems such a useless thing to do. I am so fortunate to have a brother who stays well clear of such London dens."

"Really?"

At Lord Danning's sarcastic tone, Suzanna met his gaze and frowned. "Well of course. Henry has assured me on many an occasion he does not partake in that gentlemanly pursuit."

Lord Danning manoeuvred the curricle to a halt not far from where Victoria strolled with Mr. Swinson and ordered his tiger to hold the horses.

Suzanna ignored the warm comforting heat of his lordship's hand as he helped her step from the carriage. Even the leather of her glove was no impediment to the effect he had on her. It was unlike anything she'd ever experienced before. *Damn him.*

Victoria rushed toward them. "Suzanna, I was hoping to meet you here. Lord Danning told me you were to ride with him today."

"Victoria," she said, kissing her friend's cheek. "I too am glad to see you." Suzanna looked at Mr. Swinson and smiled.

"Oh, let me introduce you. This is Mr. Swinson, a friend of my father's from New York. Mr. Swinson, this is my oldest and dearest friend, Miss Suzanna March."

TAMARA GILL

Suzanna curtsied, then immediately found her hand placed neatly on Lord Danning's arm. She met Victoria's laughing gaze and strove not to blush. The gesture, as sweet as it appeared, merely indicated his lordship was a gentleman and nothing more.

"We were about to walk down to the Serpentine. Would you care to join us?" Victoria smiled and Suzanna noted Mr. Swinson's appreciative gaze linger on her friend.

Suzanna looked to Lord Danning. He nodded. "We would be pleased to join you, Lady Victoria," he said.

They strolled the grassy bank that led to the water, the sunlight warm and comforting on their skin.

"I've heard Moncroft's ball will be a crush once again. I do not understand why he sends out so many invitations when his modest ballroom can only hold so many."

Suzanna chuckled at her friend's annoyance. "To have a crush is the thing, don't you know, Victoria," she said.

"True, I suppose, but it doesn't make for a comfortable evening."

"I wholeheartedly agree, Lady Victoria," said Mr. Swinson, his native tongue sounding foreign in the English setting. "I, for one, could think of a better way to pass an evening."

"Such as?" Lord Danning asked, the aggravation in his tone in no way veiled.

Eyebrows raised, Mr. Swinson looked at Lord Danning. Suzanna held her breath as the two men seemed to take the other's measure.

"Well, to spend a night with a select group of friends, for one." Mr. Swinson answered. "Perhaps the partaking of dancing and cards."

"Hmm." Lord Danning paused. "You run a printing company in New York, I understand. What is it that brings you to London?"

Suzanna met Victoria's eyes and noted her friend's unease over the barely disguised dislike between the two men. Had Suzanna not known better, she would think Lord Danning jealous. Did his lordship like Victoria and disagree with her association with the American? Was his denial of attraction to her friend a lie? Or was it because Mr. Swinson was in trade and therefore beneath notice?

"Pleasure, mostly." Mr. Swinson smiled at Victoria. "And to see Lord Ross, of course. As you are well aware, his lordship is an old friend of my father's. Then I shall travel to Paris. I'm looking to start a woman's fashion magazine."

"Sounds exciting," Victoria stated.

"I wish you well with your endeavours, Mr. Swinson." Suzanna smiled in all sincerity. She turned to Lord Danning. "I believe it's time I returned home, my lord."

"Of course."

Suzanna bade goodbye to her friend and promised to meet up with her that evening. They walked to the carriage in silence. She stepped up into the curricle and settled her skirts.

No sooner had she done so than the carriage lurched to one side as Lord Danning stepped within. Immediately upon him seating himself, Suzanna was reminded of how little room the carriage sported. His broad shoulders left modest space between them. With a flick of the reins, they were off.

"You never answered my question, Suzanna."

She looked away from the shop fronts gracing Park Terrace and turned to Lord Danning. A frisson of desire shot through her at his intense gaze. She stared, captured by the longing in his eyes, before pulling her attention back to the road ahead. The feelings he evoked would not do at all. They were friends and nothing more. She swallowed. "What question was that, my lord?"

"If you would waltz with me tonight? I do mean to repair the damage I caused you last season, and I think stepping out with me this eve will ensure many a gentleman will ask for your hand."

He smiled, clasped her hand, and raised it to his lips. His eyes met hers just as his lips touched her glove and Suzanna reminded herself to close her mouth.

"I'm sure this drive today has more than helped, my lord. Besides, for all we know, it may have been something other than our disagreement last season that saw the *ton* term me a failure." Suzanna paused. "In any case, it does not signify what balls and parties to which society will invite me. I am determined to marry for love and to a man who is wealthy enough not to be in the least awed by my dowry. All I have to do is find him."

"Even so," he said, flicking the ribbons once more. "Will you waltz with me?"

"Yes, of course. I would be honoured." Suzanna looked toward her home looming before them, a haven she longed to step within before she became the blabbering fool from last season. Under the intense scrutiny of his lordship, it was only a matter of time before she blundered, and said something ridiculous.

It would be so easy to fall for his ardent charm and hooded, deep, ocean-blue eyes in which any woman would be willing to drown.

CHAPTER 8

The Moncroft ball was indeed a crush. People milled in every available space of which there was little in the undersized room. Suzanna and Victoria greeted the Countess and joined the throng. Few were recognizable due to the masks and dominos covering their faces and evening wear.

Suzanna looked about the ballroom in awe. Guests disguised in an array of masks—some plain and others decorated with gems–circulated and danced with carefree abandon. Beads, silk, and jewels sparkled in the candlelit room, giving the night an air of mystery and decadence.

Excitement thrummed in her blood. Never had she been to such an event. And as much as she wished to deny her feelings, Suzanna was excited about her forthcoming waltz with Lord Danning. To have his arms about her, pulling her close to his strong physique was enough to make this evening marvellous. Even unforgettable.

"It will be impossible to know to whom we are talking. I cannot even make out some of the women's hair colour under their wigs, not to mention their faces under the masks," Victoria said, looking about.

Suzanna clasped Victoria's arm and pulled her toward an area of the room that looked to afford more space. "Did Mr. Swinson tell you what he planned to wear this eve? He is to attend, I assume?"

"Yes," Victoria said, stopping a footman and taking two glasses of champagne. "But he did not tell me what mask he would wear."

"Do you like him, Victoria?" Suzanna asked. Not that she really wanted to hear the answer, should it be yes. Poor Henry would be devastated should he lose the affection of Victoria. But as her friend, she owed Victoria the opportunity to openly share her feelings.

"I do. Of course, I do. He is pleasant and always jovial." Victoria paused, a slight frown marring her brow. "He is certainly a favourite with Papa."

Suzanna nodded. "I should imagine so."

"Between you and me, Suzanna, I do believe Papa would like me to marry him. Not that I will, of course," she hastened to add. "But Mr. Swinson, for all his American ways, is actually the Earl of Manning's heir—a distant cousin, twice removed; but still the heir when all is told."

It was all Suzanna could do to hold the lump at bay in her throat over her friend's disclosure. Henry would lose this battle just as she lost the battle to stop being clumsy at the age of eighteen. Poor Henry, he would be devastated.

A lengthy silence settled between them; one Suzanna found difficult to breach.

Finally Victoria looked at her. "Should Mr. Swinson ask for my hand, the answer will be not to his liking or my father's, Suzanna."

Suzanna blinked and met her friend's gaze, the note of conviction in Victoria's voice leaving no room for doubt of her sincerity. "I cannot tell you how relieved I am to hear such news, even if it is at the expense of Mr. Swinson and your father's happiness." She clasped Victoria's hand. "Does this mean should Henry ask for your hand in marriage you would be in agreement? That one day will I not only be able to call you my friend but my sister?"

"Yes it does," Victoria replied, "if Henry should *ever* ask. Now talking of happiness, I do believe Lord Danning is heading our way."

All the air expelled from Suzanna's lungs when Lord Danning, dressed in a double-breasted coat with two tails stalked toward them, his heavy-lidded eyes fixed on one person.

Her...

Suzanna swallowed and then swallowed again when he towered before them. Tall and without a mask, his attention was obvious to any who cared to notice. Victoria, having such impeccable manners, politely bade good evening to his lordship, then walked away.

Unable to deny herself, Suzanna curtsied and took the opportunity to ogle his lordship's muscular legs, which filled his skin-tight breeches very well. The peculiar sensation of desire shot to her lower abdomen. No matter how much she tried to deny it, Suzanna was hopelessly attracted to him.

He leaned close. "You are the epitome of beauty this eve, Miss March." His whispered words sending a shiver of delight down her spine. "May I have this dance?"

Suzanna nodded, the ability to speak having vanished. His warm, gloved hand clasped hers, and he led them onto the floor. Other guests milled about them, readying themselves for the forthcoming waltz.

It took all Suzanna's will not to swoon when his lordship's arm settled about her waist. She caught the hint of sandalwood—an earthy, rich scent—as he pulled her against him. His chest was solid, his arms strong, yet his hands were gentle as they held her.

She cleared her throat. "I'm surprised you knew me, Lord Danning? My Egyptian costume fooled even my brother." She smiled in the hope it would mask her nerves. He was an excellent dancer, his steps sure and capable as they floated around the room.

"I would know you anywhere, Suzanna," he said, leaning devilishly close, the breath of his words tickling her ear. Suzanna turned and found her mouth deliciously close to his. Their gazes collided and locked. Time seemed to stop.

"I do not recall giving you leave to use my given name, my lord?"

"Ahh, but you did, remember? In the park yesterday," he said. "So may I, Suzanna? I promise to return the favour and allow you to call me Royce when we're in private."

Lord Danning's—Royce's—gaze settled on her lips. He was so close. So close, Suzanna had only to lean forward and their mouths would meet. Memories of his ardent, seductive kiss had her yearning for another. Another taste of sin.

A shrill laugh in the room brought them both to their senses. Lord Danning leaned back and smiled before settling them once again at a more appropriate distance.

"You make me forget I'm a gentleman, Suzanna." He sighed. "You do realize before this evening is over I'm going to thoroughly kiss you again."

Suzanna chuckled and raised her brow at the surety in his voice. "Really, *Royce*? And when, pray tell, will you have the opportunity to do so? I shall not be venturing to the terrace with you this evening, and you cannot kiss me here."

"I want to kiss you. Here and now."

Suzanna wanted it, too. Just the thought of engaging in such a naughty escapade before the uppity *ton* sent her rebellious side to sing. "Well you cannot. I forbid it." She smiled and allowed herself to relax and enjoy the dance. At times, their gazes would collide and the dizzying, wonderful roll in her belly would occur. But, like all good things, the dance came to an end.

Royce, the perfect gentleman, escorted her to a quiet corner within sight of the dowager countess and her aunt Agnes, and sought out a beverage for them both. Suzanna watched him retreat and cursed the coat tails on his suit that obstructed her view.

Royce watched Suzanna sip her mulled wine. Her lips, supple and red, kissed the glass rim, and his body tightened with need. Her unique emerald eyes took in the festivities before them, the slightest smile playing upon her lips.

He marvelled at the fact Suzanna had not the slightest conception of what a beauty she was. Last season, had he had more control of his temper, he could have proven his regard for her before she fled to Paris. Now with every word he spoke, Suzanna scrutinized, and wondered if he were being honest.

He knew she wondered when he would hurt her feelings again.

Yet he played no game, other than making her his wife. With every moment he spent in her presence Royce wished for more. He wanted her under his protection and his to hold for as long as time would give them. He wanted her to be the woman to bear his children and sleep beside him for the next fifty years, if they were so fortunate.

Royce took a calming breath. To demonstrate his love to Suzanna would prove difficult. His reputation as a rake, his past treatment, and his dislike of her brother were not obstructions easily overcome.

Nor was the fact he needed a wealthy bride and soon.

He paused. *Love?* Did he love her? He smiled when she laughed at something taking place on the ballroom floor. An ache settled in his chest that could only mean one thing. He did indeed love this woman. Wanted her with a need that at times scared and excited him, but also made him complete.

"Suzanna, if you're not already engaged, may I have the supper waltz?"

She looked at him in shock before blinking, and concealing her surprise. "Two waltzes in one night, my lord? You will create talk."

Royce took delight in her smile and wished he could always create such a reaction from her. "Let the *ton* talk; they are nothing to me, whereas you, Miss March are fast becoming everything."

"You flatter me, my lord."

"If you like," he said enjoying the rosy hue that settled on her cheeks. He stepped close and slipping his hand within the folds of her domino, clasped her hand. "I'll flatter and spoil you for all time if you'd only give me a second chance, Miss March."

Her hand was delicate and warm. His thumb slid over her silk glove, eliciting a tremor that ran directly into his heart. He noted her increased breathing and met her gaze. "Please follow me, and allow me to kiss you once this night."

"You are too bold, my lord." Suzanna took a sip of her wine and turned away.

"No amount of drink will calm your nerves, my dear. The attraction between us cannot be denied." He paused. "Please, Suzanna." He would beg should he have to. It was either that or throw her over his shoulder like a ruffian and carry her out of the room against her will.

She made an indelicate sound of protest and then nodded. Royce bowed and made his way toward the supper room doors. If memory served him correctly, a door within the room led to a passage that ran the length of the ballroom. At the supper room doors, he gazed over his shoulder and noted Suzanna following him at a discreet distance.

As he made the supper room threshold, he gazed over his shoulder and hesitated as Suzanna made her way toward him. Once she made the room, he motioned her to follow him into the passage beyond.

The air in the passage, cooler than in the ballroom, did nothing to dampen his desire to taste her again.

"I'm sure someone has seen our less-than-discreet disappearance, my lord."

"Royce. And you are well hidden under the mask and domino should they have noticed. Your escape into my waiting embrace will be our little secret, Suzanna." He pulled her into a darkened room. It smelt of cleaning oils and pine. Suzanna cautiously made her way forward then halted before a lady's writing desk. She turned toward him. Royce twisted the lock on the door, the snap of bolts loud as they slid into place. Suzanna eyed him warily. He stalked toward her and stopped when her hand settled on his chest.

"Royce, I should not be here embarking on such scandalous behaviour." She stepped past him, and he clasped her arm.

"Suzanna, I will not ruin you if that is your fear." He frowned and clasped her face with his hands. Her skin was soft, her hair smelled of jasmine. Unable to wait a moment longer to gaze upon her beauty, he untied the mask. The silk ribbon fell away from her chin, and Royce allowed the mask to fall on the desk behind her.

"I'm in love with you, Suzanna March. In truth, I do believe I fell in love with you the day I saw you in that ghastly frilly gown at your coming-out last season."

He smiled at her shock and kissed her. His body heated at her ardent response to his chaste embrace and the need within his soul roared.

Royce pulled back and waited for her to look at him. He enjoyed seeing her eyes cloudy with desire. "I wish for you to trust me, Suzanna. I have been termed a rake and a scoundrel, but I have never dallied with an innocent. I wish to marry you, honour you for all of our lives, and have children with you. Please give me a chance to prove myself worthy of your love."

"Oh, Royce." Suzanna swallowed the obscenely large lump wedged in her throat. Did he truly mean what he said? Did he speak the truth, or was he merely saying such things to have his way with her?

"I don't know what to say. I...."

"Say you'll marry me and make me the happiest man in London."

Royce kissed her again and Suzanna lost all line of thought. Heaven above, his kisses, no matter how quick, were enough to befuddle her senseless. And at this moment she truly needed to keep her wits about her.

"My brother does not approve of you and I do not know if I can trust you." As much as it pained her to see his disappointment, she truly did not. He had hurt her so last year when she thought they were forming a friendship. Henry kept terming him a fortune hunter. She prayed her brother was wrong.

"May I think over your proposal, my lord?"

He nodded. "Call me Royce in private please, Suzanna. And of course you may take your time. I'll not rush your decision."

Suzanna stilled when he met her gaze, and the heat that radiated from his eyes sent her skin to burn. "May the fine lady grant her humblest servant a kiss now?"

"I believe she will." When his lips touched hers Suzanna leaned into his warmth and nestled against his chest. His heart beat fast beneath the many folds of clothing, and oddly, Suzanna had the urge to remove them. To feel his skin, taste, and kiss him all over.

Heat bloomed on her face, and she was thankful Royce had his eyes closed. She was becoming scandalous with her wayward thoughts. Every time his lips sought hers and his hands touched her flesh, it left her longing for more, and strangely unsatisfied for something she could not name.

He pulled away and gazed at her. He ran his thumb against her cheeks, and the loss of his touch, his kiss, left a hollow feeling in her chest. Suzanna swallowed and couldn't form one reason against denying him further liberties, to allow herself to love him in the most intimate of ways a woman could love a man. He loved her, had asked for her hand in marriage. Should she say yes? No one needed ever to know they'd slept together before they wed.

It was a risk, on more than one level. She could become *enceinte*. Such a scandal would force her to marry a man her brother loathed. It was all very confusing and becoming more so with every kiss Royce bestowed beneath her ear.

The wooden side of the desk touched her legs as he moved her back. Suzanna, as if she weighed no more than a leaf, was lifted upon it. Paper scrunched under her bottom. She bit her lip when Royce's hand slid her silk gown above her knee. He stepped between her legs and for the first time in her life, the desire of a man lay against her own heated flesh.

His hardness did odd things to her body. She could not touch him enough. She wanted Royce to end the sweet ache between her thighs. She pulled him closer, wanting no space between them, and touched herself against his hardness. A sigh escaped as the contact went some way to dispel her need.

"We should stop before we cannot, Suzanna."

Royce's hunger-filled plea made her decision simple. She could not stop and did not want to miss lying with a man she loved and had loved all along, if she was truthful with herself. If she refused his offer of marriage, settled into a marriage of convenience with another gentleman and if by so doing she never again experienced this fire burning through her soul, her decision to stop would be forever regretted.

Suzanna refused to live with regret. She met his gaze and untied his cravat, hoping Royce did not notice her shaking fingers. He drew in a deep breath and Suzanna read in his pained visage his inner fight between desire and conscience.

"I think," she said, sliding his coat from his shoulders and revelling in the taut muscles beneath his shirt, "it is too late to stop."

Suzanna could not tell who undressed who more

quickly; she only knew there was no time to waste. The gown she wore was no impediment to Royce's competent hands, and was soon, along with her domino, tossed onto the already discarded clothing piled at his lordship's feet. The small room enfolded them in warmth and her skin shivered in sensual awakening.

Royce came against her and pulled her close. The hair on his chest was unlike anything she had ever felt before. It tickled and tempted at the same time. Suzanna licked her lips while her gaze devoured his upper body. Her fingers traced his chest and then moved to touch the muscles that descended like a ladder toward sin. A sin she fully intended to experience.

Suzanna murmured her delight when he laid her down upon the desk. He cupped her face and kissed her hard, his tongue demanding and tangling with her own. Suzanna welcomed his vigour and replied in turn as well as she could. Cool air caressed her silk-clad leg when he rucked her shift up to her waist. She rubbed her leg against his side and he growled.

She let her legs fall open and allowed him to settle between her thighs. Her skin burned, her body begging for something unknown but was soon to find out. Suzanna moaned when his hand cupped her most sensitive flesh and stroked.

Yes....

Royce was masterful at seduction, and without doubt, the rumours she had heard about town of his prowess as a lover were correct. Royce knew how to please a woman. He stroked her sex—soft, round movements tormenting her to madness. Suzanna opened her eyes when a low, seductive chuckle tickled her ear. She kissed him and allowed herself the delight of touching his back, the muscles flexing beneath his skin with his every movement.

"I must have you." Royce shoved his breeches down and Suzanna's mouth went dry. Never had she seen a man naked. Her lips curved. It was a marvellous sight to behold.

He came over her and she tensed as his manhood—hard, yet soft as velvet—pushed against her sex.

"I'll be as gentle as I can, my love."

Suzanna nodded and tried to relax. He eased into her; a strange and foreign pressure unlike anything she'd ever experienced. Then in one swift slide, he breached her maidenhead.

She gasped and swallowed a sob. A sharp pain tore through her sex and then settled to a light ache.

Within moments, the pain dissipated and where he now laid a new type of ache began—an ache similar to before but more powerful and urgent. Excitement over the unknown sensations Royce was eliciting tickled across her skin. Then he shifted his weight and moved, and comprehension dawned.

Suzanna's axis tilted.

Her hands slid to his buttocks and she squeezed. Sweat pooled upon his skin. She rubbed where her fingernails bit into his skin and kissed his neck and his chest.

"Marry me, Suzanna." Royce sought her lips and teased her with small beckoning kisses. "Please...."

To ask her at such a time was unfair, and yet all Suzanna could think was *yes*. How could a sane modern woman live without a husband like him? He was gentle, kind, and brought her body to life whenever he was present.

To walk away from such passion would surely be a mistake. Royce may not love her yet or more truthfully, she may not believe in his love at this very moment; but in time, with the sort of passion that sparked between them whenever they were together love was not impossible.

She gazed up at him, his sensual movements pushing her towards a cliff she couldn't climb fast enough. She saw hunger, passion, and fear in the window to his soul.

His fingers flexed against her bottom, and he rocked into her deep and hard. "Yes," she moaned. His movements threw her over an edge, and she fell into a void of utter bliss.

He allowed her to catch her breath before he asked, "Yes, you will marry me? Or yes, you're enjoying what we're doing on this desk?"

Suzanna smiled, but didn't reply to his teasing. Royce groaned and kissed the arch of her neck, sending tingles to race across her skin. He pushed within her, his body tensing, his own release as powerful as hers.

He untangled them and came to lie beside her, his hand cupping his head as he gazed at her. Suzanna clasped his cheek and ran her fingers against the short stubble on his jaw before letting her hand drop to her side. "I will marry you, Lord Danning."

His smile lit a spark within her soul extinguished twelve months ago. How strange life was. For months she had denied her feelings, kept them hidden under anger, and intentions of revenge.

But forgiveness and love trumped blame and hate. Soon she would be his wife. Lady Danning.

She grinned. The masquerade ball had been a magical evening indeed.

CHAPTER 9

Suzanna all but floated down the staircase in her brother's Mayfair home the following morning, unable to shift the smile from her lips. After making love with Royce, all her concerns and worries seemed to have vanished. He had asked for her hand and wished to marry her.

And she had said yes.

Suzanna hugged the wonder of it to herself and smiled at the footman who held open the breakfast room door. Thoughts of their forthcoming wedding day overran her mind. Since she had lain with him, the sooner they wed the better, just in case a little Lord Danning was already growing in her womb.

Love and longing filled her mind, and Suzanna couldn't wait to start the new life offered to her last night. After they had left the sanctuary of the small room, Royce had assured her he would call on her brother this morning to formally ask for her hand.

Suzanna frowned down at the eggs she was piling on her plate. Henry would react badly to the news. It was no secret he loathed Royce due to his previous treatment of her. But as she had seen fit to forgive it left her brother with no reason for ill will.

"Leave some for me. Have an appetite this morning, do you?" Henry came to stand beside her and looked over the sideboard.

Heat bloomed on Suzanna's cheeks, and she hastily added a slice of toast to her plate before sitting at the table. "Balls always leave me starved the morning after." Suzanna sipped her tea. "Do you have any plans this morning, Henry?"

Henry settled at the head of the table, and gave her a searching look. "I had a letter early this morning from Lord Danning. Seems he wants to meet with me at my earliest convenience. He should arrive at eleven."

Suzanna feigned surprise and nodded. "Do you know what about?" Butterflies took flight in her stomach at the thought.

"No. Not yet. But I'm sure I will soon enough." Henry cleared his throat. "Lord Danning has also asked for you to be present, Suzanna. Should I be worried about what is to be discussed in my library?"

Unable or perhaps unwilling to lie to her dearest brother, Suzanna shrugged lest she say anything that could throw her brother into an early temper. Such a reaction would be soon upon them once Royce formally asked for her hand, followed by her acceptance of such a request.

Silence settled between them like a cloak of doom. Henry was no fool and from the scowl upon his face, he appeared well aware of what was to come.

Suzanna steeled herself. It wasn't as if Henry was going to marry Royce and live with him. She was. So surely her brother would see past his own hatred of the man and let her be. Perhaps one day, even be happy for her.

She hoped.

※

By the time Royce arrived, Suzanna's nerves were frazzled and taut as a harp's string. Henry had chosen not to quiz her on the purpose of his lordship's visit, yet with a sinking feeling she knew there was no need. Her brother was no simpleton and no doubt had already worded his rejection of Lord Danning's suit to his sister.

At the sound of a knock on the library door, Suzanna turned. "Lord Danning to see you Mr. March," the butler said.

"Come forward, Lord Danning," Henry replied, his voice devoid of warmth.

Silently she watched as Royce moved across the room, and at Henry's curt gesture, seated himself beside her in front of Henry's desk. Dressed in a morning suit, Lord Danning had an air of elegance and ease. But his hands clasped tightly at his sides betrayed the disquiet running through him. Her heart tweaked a little knowing he wanted her enough to be nervous about the meeting.

Danning's wink and knowing smile nudged some of her apprehension away before her brother's brisk cold welcome brought her back to reality. Suzanna braced herself for the imminent question.

"You wished to see us, Lord Danning?" Henry gestured for him to begin and made a point of looking disinterested in the Viscount's presence.

"I've come here this morning, March, to formally ask for Suzanna's hand in marriage. A request I believe your sister is happy to receive and agree."

Henry nodded, his eyes as cold as ice chips. Without

moving his gaze from his lordship he asked, "Is this correct, Suzanna? You wish to marry Lord Danning?"

Suzanna looked at the two men she loved most in her life and wondered how she could make them allies instead of enemies, yet all the while she knew her next words would only increase her brother's animosity. "Yes. I wish to marry Lord Danning."

Suzanna met Royce's gaze and smiled. She blinked back tears from the overwhelming love blossoming in her chest as Royce clasped her fingers and kissed her hand.

Henry laughed. "I will not allow it. Frankly I'm surprised I allowed such a low-life cad as Lord Danning to enter our home. I will neither grant my blessing nor allow my sister to marry you, my lord. Now," Henry said, standing, "this interview is over. You may leave."

Suzanna frowned. "Henry, don't be so rude. I'm of age. Please do not make me marry Lord Danning without your approval. For I will. You know I will." She matched her brother's cold stare with one of her own.

"You will not, for I believe Lord Danning has not been as honest with you as he should. Would you care to enlighten my sister as to why you wish to marry her or should I?"

"Henry, I know not of what you speak but please stop this nonsense and be happy for me," Suzanna pleaded.

"Well, Danning?" Henry said, ignoring her.

"I love Suzanna; what more is there to say?" Royce smiled over to her but the light in his blue orbs had dimmed and dread clawed at her innards.

"Since you're unwilling to be truthful, allow me." Henry met her gaze. "I had hoped to spare you this pain, Suzanna. I truly did. I tried to warn you. But, I would never willingly hurt you and what I'm about to disclose I fear will hurt you immensely."

He threw down his quill. "It was one of the reasons why I welcomed your moving in a completely different set to Lord Danning and his calibre of friends for I hoped you would meet a man worthy of your heart. But," he sighed, "it seems my wish has not been granted."

"Say what you will, Henry," Suzanna said, all hope of her brother and Royce becoming friends fading to an impossible dream.

"At the beginning of last year's season, I attended a gambling den in the bowels of East London where I had the opportune delight, I would say, of playing Lord Danning's younger brother in a game of cards."

"Now what started out as a simple game of Piquet soon turned into a game of high stakes." Henry stood and marched to the window, his gaze on the street for a time. "I won, of course, George Durnham's inebriation and lack of concentration enabled me to win a sizable fortune from him. Of course, he signed a vowel, and I thought to receive payment in a week or two."

"I forgot all about the money he owed me until the night he started to spout off in Whites how he believed my sister had a tendre for his brother, and what a fool she was to think herself equal to such a match." Henry's eyes narrowed on Royce. "I should not have allowed the little fool to vex me, yet he did; and so I challenged him to a second game of cards. All or nothing. It was a challenge no gambling enthusiast could refuse."

Royce's hands clenched in his lap.

"I triumphed again over George Durnham. His lordship's brother wrote another vowel at my agreement. It was only when I received word of Lord Danning's cold and callous treatment of you that I demanded payment in full. For too long we've been shadows in the *ton* due to our family's heritage. The opportunity arose and I seized our revenge."

"Henry, what happened between me and Lord Danning was all a misunderstanding. Why do you continue to bring...?"

"Let me finish, Suzanna."

She remained silent and looked to Royce for support only to see him scowling at her brother.

"I demanded payment. Money I knew neither Lord Danning nor his brother had. For months I have been pulling the noose tighter about their necks. I am within my rights to obtain the money owed to me." Henry shrugged. "That the viscount's family has fallen on hard times is not my concern. But now as the head of the family and knowing Lord Danning wishes to marry my heiress sister, that," Henry said, striding back to the desk, and leaning over it, "concerns me greatly."

Suzanna was stunned into silence, not knowing how to react to such news. Her brother, for all his faults, was not normally a revengeful person. Yet after many months of snubs and exclusion from Lord Danning's set, perhaps her even-tempered brother had been pushed too far. As for Royce being out of funds, this was a shocking revelation. Not that she cared if he were poor, but more because he had hidden it from her.

An awful thought crawled into her mind. All the dances, the teasing remarks, and stolen kisses were an act and a way for Royce to make her fall in love with him so she'd marry him. And she had done exactly that—fallen for a man who was only after one thing.

Her wealth.

Suzanna met Lord Danning's gaze. "Are you penniless?"

He reached for her hand, and Suzanna pulled away.

He ran a hand through his hair and glared at her brother. "For years I have been trying to stop my brother from gambling and living a life of ill repute. But, alas, such actions were of no use. He continued to live a life well beyond his means."

"To keep the family name from being tarnished, I paid all the debts he accumulated. I continued to pay his bills and living expenses wherever they arose, here in England or on the continent. But the sum he owed your brother was too much. I could not pay it. I myself am to blame also. I have a tendency to love horseflesh, racing, and carriages. Not to mention my estate in Rome costs a fortune to upkeep while remaining empty for years on end. I admit I have not been wise with the Danning fortune."

"I've sold everything not entailed but it has barely dented the debt." Lord Danning sat forward in his chair and faced her. Suzanna looked at the floor, unable to look at him.

"I requested an extension from your brother, asking for time and received a curt and immovable refusal from his solicitor."

Suzanna looked at Henry and noted the hardened look of a man hell-bent on revenge. Bile rose in her throat.

"It is true, Suzanna," Lord Danning continued, "I was advised at the beginning of the season to marry an heiress. And it is exactly what I set out to do until I saw you back in London and looking as delightful as ever. I fell in love with you again." Lord Danning stood and lifted her chin to meet his gaze. "The night I shunned you was the night I found out my brother owed your brother a sum I knew I could not pay. I was in a temper and lashed out. You just happened to be the unfortunate person to encounter me at such an importune time. I apologized for my behaviour and ill humour before, and I will do so again. You did not deserve it."

Suzanna swallowed the lump in her throat and blinked back tears.

"Yet you still lie, Lord Danning. For months you have been gloating over the love my sister has held for you. Do not deny this. I imagine the idea of my own family's money paying off your debt to me filled your heart with selfish glee."

"Money and debt aside, you have never liked me, March, and out-manoeuvring you was not my aim. My financial situation did not change how I feel. I welcomed Suzanna's love and nothing in my past changes the fact I love her in return."

Suzanna looked from one to the other, not knowing whom to believe, nor wanting to listen to any more of this sordid story.

Time. She needed time to figure out what her heart and mind were warring about. Did Lord Danning love her or her money? That her brother would seek such revenge on any man was a sobering thought. This was certainly not the way they had been raised.

Time.

She took a deep breath and let it out slowly. But her heart still raced. "Lord Danning, in light of what has been said this day, I'm sorry but I cannot marry you."

Henry smiled. "I guess you should be leaving as it appears your business with our family is over, Lord Danning."

"Shut up, Henry," Suzanna snapped.

Lord Danning clasped her shoulders. "Don't do this, Suzanna. If you believe I would marry you only for your money we can have the marriage settlement signed over to you. In fact, shun your family's wealth and marry me as penniless as I am. But do not refuse to be my wife. I love you—only you and not your money."

Suzanna bit her lip, her mind a whir of thoughts. She shook her head. "I cannot. I need time to think. I'm sorry."

Without a backward glance, she fled the room. The despair on Lord Danning's face broke her heart. Yet was it the pain of losing her or a pain brought out by the fact he no longer stood to inherit her thousands of pounds?

That she could not answer.

CHAPTER 10

Months passed, and with it came the end of the 1811 season. Suzanna gratefully farewelled it and welcomed the fact she no longer had to attend parties and balls, pretending to be happy with her lot in life.

She was not.

In truth, she was terribly depressed and not at all sure she had made the correct decision with Lord Danning just twelve weeks ago.

Her brother continued to carry on as if nothing out of the ordinary had passed between them. It vexed her greatly. For all of Lord Danning's faults, he had made no fewer mistakes than her brother. Both, she'd decided, were as bad as the other. Revenge and tempers were two traits men should never combine; it only made for unhappy endings.

Her situation was a prime example.

Suzanna flopped onto the settee and sighed. Warmth from the fire warmed her skin, yet the unfulfilled desire to see Lord Danning again, to talk to him, left her cold and empty.

Strange, but Lord Danning for the final weeks of the season had not been about in society. Suzanna had made quiet inquiries as to his whereabouts and was told he'd travelled abroad for the sale of one of his properties. Yet an inkling inside told her that this was an untruth and it gnawed at her conscience.

Where was he?

"Suzanna? Breakfast is ready. Are you not joining me?"

Suzanna looked up at her brother, noting the time. "I didn't hear the gong." She stood to join him. "Lost in thought, that is all." She walked to the door and paused on the threshold. "Henry, have you seen or heard from Lord Danning over the last few weeks?"

Her brother started and then shook his head while holding out his arm for her to take. "No. Why would I care what Lord Danning is about?"

His tone held a nervous, guilt-ridden tinge and all of Suzanna's fears surfaced.

"You know something. Where is he, Henry? I demand you tell me at once." Suzanna paused in the foyer and slid her hand from his arm. Her brother kept his face averted and refused to meet her gaze. What did he know?

"Where the blackguard deserves to be."

Suzanna stood, shocked, and watched her retreating brother's back before she collected her thoughts and ran after him, pulling him to a stop inside the breakfast room.

"Tell me what you set out to achieve has not come to fruition?" Suzanna braced herself for a truth she couldn't comprehend nor believe possible from a much-loved brother.

"Lord Danning is currently serving time in Marshalsea Prison. I suppose I should give the wretch credit for not fleeing England like his brother, doing the correct thing by his creditors, and paying for his crime. Of course, while he is in prison, I'll never see the money rightfully owed to me by his sibling."

Had Suzanna not tried so very hard to convert herself into a lady these last few months, she could well box her brother about the ears at this very moment. As it was, it took all her control for her next words not to be shrieked like a banshee.

"Lord Danning is serving time...in prison. How could you, Henry?" Suzanna stormed from the room and yelled for the footman to have the coach brought around immediately.

Not one more second would she allow Royce to suffer the hell of living in a prison. Her mind whirred as to what her actions meant, but also, as a woman, how she could go about freeing his lordship.

She frowned then turned back to the breakfast room, annoyed further by her brother as he spooned large mouthfuls of ham into his unrepentant mouth.

"Get up. You're coming with me and you'll help me have Lord Danning freed. I know your desire to punish him has led to his current situation. You were raised as a gentleman, Henry. Father would be sorely disappointed in you, first, for gambling, and second, for being such an arse as to send a man to prison without a care."

Henry's fork clattered to the table. "I will not help you free him. Had it not been me, it would have been someone else who placed him in his current situation. Anyway, why should you care? I thought your infatuation with Lord Danning was over. Did you not play with him this last season, securing your own shallow revenge?" Henry sipped his coffee, brows raised mockingly. "I am not the only one who has succeeded in their game, it would seem."

Suzanna allowed guilt to swamp her. What Henry said was indeed true. She had allowed her temper to get the better of her. She had led Royce on a merry chase and tricked him into believing she welcomed his attentions when all along she wanted to cause him pain and humiliation.

But it had not been long before his charm, apology, and his constant attention toward her had broken away the stone that surrounded her heart and allowed it to beat once more. She had fallen in love with him again but only to turn her back on him when he needed her the most. For Royce to go to prison instead of jumping into a marriage with one of the multitude of heiresses gracing town proved beyond any doubts his love was true.

He loved her.

A smile quirked her lips. "I'm marrying Lord Danning, Henry. Today I will figure out a way to release his lordship and then I'm going to Gretna Green. Don't try and stop me or I will box you about the ears like I wish to."

Henry stood and threw down his napkin. "The hell you will, Suzanna. I forbid it."

With clenched teeth, Suzanna glared. "I doubt Victoria will be at all pleased the man she thought she knew and loved could act in such a callous manner. To first place a gentleman in debtor's prison—a gentleman, might I add, who Victoria counts as a friend—then to let him rot there without mentioning it to me is unpardonable especially when you are in a position to free him.

"Secondly, Victoria will not be at all pleased her best friend and closest confidante will end heartbroken because of an elder sibling who is too pigheaded to allow her to marry the man she loves. Perhaps I was wrong in voicing my approval of you to her, especially as Mr. Swinson has been chasing her skirts all season." Suzanna tapped her chin. "American he may be, but...perhaps he is a more suitable alliance for her family after all."

"Go," Henry said, his face turning a pasty shade of white at her threat. "In my desk you'll find the blunt to pay off the warden and free Lord Danning. It would be best, I think if you retired to Lord Danning's country estate until next season. I will ensure no word of you freeing Lord Danning reaches the matron's wagging tongues." A pained expression crossed Henry's face. "Damn it. I'm coming with you. If you're to marry the blackguard, let me give you respectability until you leave London."

"Sounds quite perfect," Suzanna said, smiling. "I do love you, Henry, never doubt my affections for you but you must let me lead my own life. And no matter what you think I will be happy."

Suzanna turned and marched toward the library, the snort of disbelief the only reply she received. Never mind; he would forgive her and eventually accept Lord Danning as family.

It may take some months or perhaps years, but it would occur. "Marshalsea Prison," she yelled out to the coachman a few minutes later, her pocket a great deal heavier with coin.

"Right you are, Miss March."

Suzanna smiled at the coachman's dubious look at her brother and wondered what other facial expression he could produce when she led Lord Danning out of the prison, and commanded him to Gretna.

It was certainly something to look forward to.

She chuckled.

CHAPTER 11

Royce looked about the long, rectangular courtyard. The cold from the stone walls, starved of sunlight and allowed dampness to settle on his clothes. Clothes that after a month smelled more putrid than some of the inlets off the Thames.

He watched a woman collect water from the prison's only water supply, a hand pump in the middle of the courtyard, and sighed. His life was a disaster although no one at least could say he did not honour his debts.

It was some consolation that his stay here would be of a short duration. His steward had assured him only last week the crops were looking healthy and almost ready for harvesting. With the money due in from the sale of his private home in Rome, Henry March would be paid off, and his time in Marshalsea would be over. If only his investment in the East India Company and the Indiaman *Arniston* would dock safely and profitably, his stay would be even shorter.

The sound of the metal gates opening brought his attention toward the forecourt. Royce watched a turnkey escort a hooded figure into the prison—another poor soul unable to pay their way in society. He looked away and prayed the harvest would come soon and with it his release. Prison life, he'd found, did not suit his temperament nor standard of living at all.

"Lord Danning, you have a visitor."

Royce stood and the blood drained from his face. "Suzanna, what in God's name are you doing here? This is no place for a lady."

She looked like an angel, but some of the spark in her green orbs dimmed when she gazed upon the shoeless child playing around his mother's skirt. "I've come to apologize on behalf of my brother and myself. I was not told you were here."

He clasped her hand. Her soft skin mocked him over a lifestyle lost. Well, not for long. He had fallen low to be sure, but he was determined to pull himself out of this financial mess. "You have nothing to apologize for, Suzanna. My family's situation is my burden to bear."

"That may be so," she said, pulling him to sit beside her on the bench. "But I feel the actions of our brothers, mine in particular, have positioned you where you are this day. I am sorry for it."

Royce smiled and breathed in her clean scent. Suzanna smelled fresh, her skin porcelain white, yet her cheeks had a rosy hue from the cold yard in which they sat. "I do thank you for coming but you should leave. I would hate for you to catch a chill on my account."

"Lord Danning," she said, gazing at him in seriousness. "What you said that day in my brother's library about being in love with me. Was it true?"

Royce frowned. "Do not doubt me, Suzanna. Every word I spoke was true, *is* still true. I so love you and think of you often." She was his first thought in the morning and the last one at night.

Tears welled in her emerald orbs, and Royce had an overwhelming urge to comfort her. But he did not. The last thing Suzanna needed at this moment was a comforting hug from a man who reeked of the cesspit.

"I do not doubt you, Royce, and I'm glad to hear you were in earnest. Now," she said, standing, "come, gather whatever you wish to take. We have a carriage waiting."

Royce looked up at her and wondered for a moment if the love of his life had lost her wits since walking through the prison gates. "I cannot leave, Suzanna. I have debts still to pay and some months yet to serve. As much as I would love to flee with you, you must see 'tis not possible."

"Yes it is," she said, pulling her kid leather gloves back on, a twinkle of mischief in her gaze. "I've paid the turnkey a sizable sum, of which I'm sure he is informing the warden at this moment. Your debts with my brother no longer stand. So when you're ready you are free to go."

Royce watched Suzanna stroll off toward the exit and then quickly caught up to her determined strides. "I will not allow you to pay my debts and free me. That is not the way of a gentleman."

She nodded then surprised him by leaning forward and kissing him full on the lips. Heat stole through his body at the gesture and it took all of his control not to clasp her tight against him and cover her in all his grime.

"And I refuse to allow the man I love to rot in prison due to two brothers who should've known better. I know you are not entirely responsible for your family's debt. Our brothers are to blame, and I will not allow my future husband to sit in Marshalsea because of it. Must I wait months to wed you? Of course, if it would make you feel any better you may pay me back with interest." She quirked her lips and strolled off again.

How he loved her. A strong, determined little minx was his Suzanna, and she would marry him. Had said she loved him. Never before had he wanted to exclaim his joy in front of all and sundry. "So you will marry me, Miss March?" Royce yelled out.

"Of course," she said over her shoulder before stopping to wait for him. "But if you do not hurry up, Lord Danning, I may change my mind."

Royce laughed, caught up to Suzanna, and kissed her soundly. The sound of laughter and jibes from the other prisoners soon faded, replaced by the undeniable passion and love that sang between them.

He reluctantly pulled away and went to collect his meagre belongings before joining Suzanna at the gate. "We will go to your brother directly. I will demand he give us his blessings and we'll be married immediately."

"There's no need. I've already told Henry I'm going to marry you with or without his approval. And I'm not going home in any case. We're for Gretna. Henry, in fact, is headed home right at this moment and sending my maid to meet up with us along the way. Your valet will be with her when they arrive."

"Gretna?" Royce followed her to the enclosed carriage parked before the prison and handed his bag to the waiting coachman. "What are you up to, Suzanna?"

"Nothing too scandalous, I promise you. We're for Gretna, where you'll marry me with the help of a smithy and his anvil."

Royce helped Suzanna climb into the carriage and followed her, seating himself beside her on the squabs. "You're serious?"

"Yes. Very. Now, make yourself comfortable, we have

over three hundred miles to travel." She scrunched up her nose. "However, at the first opportunity we will find an inn for you to wash."

Royce laughed and clasped her hand, wondering if the rest of his life would be as full of surprise. He found himself in awe of the wondrous woman who sat beside him. Somehow he knew life would never be dull.

※

It took only a few days to reach Gretna. The Great North Road was one Suzanna never wished to travel again. Long and arduous, the journey seemed to take forever, especially when one was looking forward to reaching their destination and marrying the man one loved.

A very vexing man, she was starting to think. Not once while alone in the carriage had he tried to compromise his future bride. Kisses he bestowed and willingly; but as heated as they became, her future husband would pull away, sit her back in the squabs and talk of the countryside or his estate.

He was driving her insane.

They were due to arrive in Gretna within the hour, and hopefully be married forthwith. Excitement and butterflies rolled in her belly over the hours to come. From this night forward, there would no longer be separate bedchambers. Tonight. Finally. Royce would take her in his arms and make her truly his.

Suzanna gazed at his profile as he took in the outskirts of Gretna. From the days of travel, a heavy stubble had formed on his cheeks and jaw which left him so unlike the man he was in London. Usually meticulously attired according to the *ton's* standard, now he sat beside her, cravat undone and shirt creased from sitting too long in his bag.

It didn't detract from his good looks. If anything, the dark, dishevelled appearance suited him. Perhaps she would ask him to keep his unshaven form.

The carriage rocked to a halt. Suzanna looked out the window and spied a whitewashed, stone building with a thatch roof. Single story and basic in design, Suzanna absorbed the location where she would marry her viscount.

"We're here. Are you ready to be my wife?"

Suzanna leant toward Royce and pulled him close for a kiss. Having learned from him what one should do when kissing, she opened for him and deepened the embrace. Royce tensed then with a growl, followed suit and pushed her back against the squabs taking her lips in a fearsome way.

Fire coursed through her blood. Her hands clasped the hair at his nape. If his kisses were anything to go by, tonight would be more memorable than the last.

She sighed as he pulled away.

"What are you sighing about?" Royce met her gaze, his eyes burning with unsated lust.

"I was merely thinking tonight we'll be husband and wife and all that it entails."

He quirked his eyebrow and smiled. "Indeed we will."

Royce helped her alight from the carriage and ushered her into the smithy. Within minutes, he had procured the services of the blacksmith and witnesses for their union. The marriage took less than fifteen minutes. Suzanna and Royce spoke their vows and with the clang of the hammer and payment of a few guineas she became Lady Danning.

"I love you, wife."

"And I you, husband."

The next morning, Suzanna slumped against the multitude of pillows in her bed at a local inn. She looked about the room the innkeeper had explained was for newlyweds. Native flowers sat in a vase upon the windowsill. Two chairs faced the hearth, and the bed she now occupied was big enough for a king.

A smile quirked her lips and she shuffled under the covers. Last night had been marvellous. And to think she could sleep with Royce every night, for the rest of her life, seemed a dream come true. One would wish never to get out of bed.

A knock on the door sounded and Suzanna looked about for him. "Come in," she said, pulling the blankets higher on her person.

A maid carrying a tray entered and curtsied. "Morning, my lady. Lord Danning wished me to inform you he'll be back post-haste but wanted you to have a hearty breakfast."

The aromas of ham, eggs, and tea filled the room, and Suzanna's stomach grumbled.

"Thank you. Place it on the table before the fire if you please."

"Yes, my lady."

When the maid left, Suzanna wrapped her cloak about her shoulders and sat in the armchair before the hearth. She ate with zeal, the plain food tasting like a feast.

"Suzanna?"

She turned and smiled as Royce came into the room. "Good morning, husband."

He laughed and came and sat on the opposite chair to hers. "I wish to speak with you. Have you finished your repast?"

Suzanna placed down her napkin. "Yes, thank you. What is it you wish to say?"

Royce pulled from his coat pocket a folded missive.

"Is it from Henry? Has something happened?"

He waved her concerns away. "No. Nothing of that nature. What I wished to discuss is in relation to us."

He paused at her worried frown. "Go on," she said.

"Suzanna, as you know, my family is no longer flush with cash. George's gambling and our irresponsible lifestyle have brought the Durnhams to the brink of financial ruin."

"Yes." Suzanna nodded, not understanding why Royce would bring this up now. She was wealthy enough for both of them. He no longer had to worry about debts.

"Prior to my stay in Marshalsea, I had a marriage contract drawn up between us. I've sent a copy to London for your brother to approve and sign. This is your copy."

"What does it say?" Suzanna held her hand out for the paper clutched tightly in his hands. She unfolded it and read it as quickly as she could. "This wasn't necessary, Royce," she said meeting his gaze. "Why did you do this?"

"It was right for me to prove to you and your family that my love is for you only and not your wealth. This had to be done."

"I never doubted it, my love."

"And you never will. Your dowry is to remain your own to do with as you wish. I received word from my steward the week you arrived at Marshalsea that the home farms are doing well, and our crops look to be plentiful this year. The sale of my Rome property has finalized. All I need now are my investments in the East India Company to pay, and I should break even.

"I am determined to pay back what I owe your brother, along with other debts George has accumulated without touching your money. If I wanted to marry for such security, I could have asked any one of the chits flush with cash looking for a titled husband. But I did not. Honour and love would not allow me to."

Tears streamed down Suzanna's face. She was sure she could not love someone as much as she loved Royce right at this moment. She tore up the contract.

"What are you doing?" He leaped forward, but Suzanna had already thrown the document into the fire.

"I do not need a piece of paper to remind me I have a loving husband. I trust and believe your love is true. And you forget, Royce, in my family, when it comes to my dowry I have the choice as to how I spend it."

He kneeled before her and hugged her about the waist. "And how do you intend doing so, my lady?"

Suzanna kissed him. "By ensuring our family is never bothered with trivial debts again. By bestowing on your brother an income, should he exceed it, will lead to his spending time in Marshalsea instead of his brother. By keeping a close eye on your horseflesh expenditure and perhaps the hiring of a nanny would be a good idea."

Royce frowned. "We have no need for a nanny." He paused. "Unless...."

"Unless I'm with a child?" Suzanna smiled at her husband's shocked countenance.

"You're pregnant?" he asked.

Her hand clasped her stomach, the small round hardness low on her abdomen declaring it indeed was so. "Yes."

"But when?" he frowned. "Not last night."

"No," she laughed, "the night of the masquerade ball."

"Oh, Suzanna." Royce lifted her and kissed her soundly.

Joy unlike any she'd ever known or thought to ever have assailed her. She was in love and married to a wonderful man who loved her in return. And now a child from this magnificent affection grew in her womb.

"I will strive to be the best husband and father in London. I promise you this."

Suzanna kissed him and wiped away his tears. "You already are."

FEED AN AUTHOR, LEAVE A REVIEW

If you enjoyed the SCANDALOUS LONDON books 1-3, and would like to tell other readers your thoughts on the book, then please consider leaving a review at your preferred online bookstore or Goodreads.

LORDS OF LONDON SERIES
AVAILABLE NOW!

Dive into these charming historical romances! In this six-book series by Tamara Gill, Darcy seduces a virginal duke, Cecilia's world collides with a roguish marquess, Katherine strikes a deal with an unlucky earl and Lizzy sets out to conquer a very wicked Viscount. These stories plus more adventures in the Lords of London series!

ALSO BY TAMARA GILL

Kiss the Wallflower series
A MIDSUMMER KISS
A KISS AT MISTLETOE
A KISS IN SPRING
TO FALL FOR A KISS
KISS THE WALLFLOWER - BOOKS 1-3 BUNDLE

League of Unweddable Gentlemen Series
FROM FRANCE, WITH LOVE
HELLION AT HEART
DARE TO BE SCANDALOUS
TO BE WICKED WITH YOU
KISS ME DUKE

Lords of London Series
TO BEDEVIL A DUKE
TO MADDEN A MARQUESS
TO TEMPT AN EARL
TO VEX A VISCOUNT
TO DARE A DUCHESS
TO MARRY A MARCHIONESS
LORDS OF LONDON - BOOKS 1-3 BUNDLE
LORDS OF LONDON - BOOKS 4-6 BUNDLE

To Marry a Rogue Series

ONLY AN EARL WILL DO
ONLY A DUKE WILL DO
ONLY A VISCOUNT WILL DO

A Time Traveler's Highland Love Series
TO CONQUER A SCOT
TO SAVE A SAVAGE SCOT

Time Travel Romance
DEFIANT SURRENDER
A STOLEN SEASON

Scandalous London Series
A GENTLEMAN'S PROMISE
A CAPTAIN'S ORDER
A MARRIAGE MADE IN MAYFAIR
SCANDALOUS LONDON - BOOKS 1-3 BUNDLE

High Seas & High Stakes Series
HIS LADY SMUGGLER
HER GENTLEMAN PIRATE
HIGH SEAS & HIGH STAKES - BOOKS 1-2 BUNDLE

Daughters Of The Gods Series
BANISHED-GUARDIAN-FALLEN
DAUGHTERS OF THE GODS - BOOKS 1-3 BUNDLE

ABOUT THE AUTHOR

Tamara is an Australian author who grew up in an old mining town in country South Australia, where her love of history was founded. So much so, she made her darling husband travel to the UK for their honeymoon, where she dragged him from one historical monument and castle to another.

A mother of three, her two little gentlemen in the making, a future lady (she hopes) and a part-time job keep her busy in the real world, but whenever she gets a moment's peace she loves to write romance novels in an array of genres, including regency, medieval and time travel.

www.tamaragill.com
tamaragillauthor@gmail.com

Printed in Poland
by Amazon Fulfillment
Poland Sp. z o.o., Wrocław